The MAGNIFICENT

Lizzie Brown

VICKI LOCKWOOD

Books in
THE MAGNIFICENT LIZZIE BROWN
series

THE MYSTERIOUS PHANTOM

THE DEVIL'S HOUND

THE GHOST SHIP

THE FAIRY CHILD

The MAGNIFICENT Lizzie Brown

AND THE MYSTERIOUS PHANTOM

VICKI LOCKWOOD

First published in 2014 by Curious Fox,
an imprint of Capstone Global Library Limited,
7 Pilgrim Street, London, EC4V 6LB
Registered company number: 6695582

www.curious-fox.com

Text © Hothouse Fiction Ltd 2014

Series created by Hothouse Fiction
www.hothousefiction.com

The author's moral rights are hereby asserted.

Cover design by Jo Hinton-Malivoire.

ISBN 978 1 78202 064 6

18 17 16 15 14
1 3 5 7 9 10 8 6 4 2

A CIP catalogue for this book is available from the British Library.

Typeset in Adobe Garamond Pro by Hothouse Fiction Ltd

Printed and bound by CPI Group (UK) Ltd, Croydon, CR0 4YY

With special thanks to
Kate Cary and Adrian Bott

CHAPTER 1

'Ain't you up yet, girl?'

Pa's iron grip jerked Lizzie awake.

'All right, all right!' Lizzie shook him off and kicked free of her ragged blanket. She swung her legs over the side of her rough wooden bed and stuck her feet into her boots.

Dawn light filtered through rags pinned over the window. The cracked door to their tiny room was still swinging where Pa had barged through.

He was carrying a package wrapped in tattered newspaper. For a foolish moment, Lizzie wondered if he'd been out to fetch her a present. Perhaps he'd brought a nice bit of mackerel. That would be a proper treat – it would make a change from yesterday's dry bread.

Pa slammed the package down on the table. Lizzie guessed from the clunk that it was a bottle of gin and her heart sank.

'Are you drinkin' already?' she muttered.

'I'll need somethin' to keep me insides warm while I'm out there earnin' enough to keep you.' Pa flung a resentful frown at her as he sat on the edge of his bunk and began rolling up his trouser legs. 'Give me the soap and fetch down the vinegar. I'm using the Scaldrum Dodge today. Be quick, lazy-legs. I want to catch the swells on their way to work.'

Lizzie jumped to her feet and grabbed the soap from its dish, then passed it to Pa. As she stood on tiptoes to reach the jar of vinegar above, she had to push aside the bright streamers of coloured paper which she'd pinned behind the rafters the night before, safely out of sight. The sixpence she'd earned doing laundry for Mrs Buckle had been enough to buy all she needed to make paper flowers. A trayful of handmade posies might earn enough to get a room of her own somewhere far away from here.

Lizzie lived in Rat's Castle, London's filthiest slum. It was thick with thieves and choked by stench. Houses leaned against each other and the tiny alleys between them were no more than sewers. Dead ends, courts and yards forked this way and that, with passages below and walkways above that felons could run through like vermin. To Lizzie it had always been home, but she found life there unbearable.

There were six children in the room next to Lizzie and Pa's, with a mother and grandmother all crammed into two beds and only an oil lamp between them. Lizzie could hear them now, the baby wailing with hunger, the children squabbling and the grandmother screeching curses at her daughter. Upstairs, men snored and grunted, sleeping off the drink that had them roaring most of the night.

The bright streamers fluttered above her, whispering the promise of a new life. She smiled to herself.

'What you smirkin' at?' Pa broke into Lizzie's dream and she nearly dropped the vinegar. She knew that tone of voice. It was dangerous.

'Nothing, Pa.' She slid the jar onto the table, but to her horror she saw that her streamers had caught his eye.

'What you want that nonsense for?' Pa began to rub soap thickly over his shins. 'Wastin' good money.'

'It ain't wasted, Pa,' Lizzie argued. 'I'm gonna make flowers to sell to the toffs on Rotten Row.'

'Lot of hard work.' Pa's legs were streaked yellow with soap. 'Why work when you can turn your hand to some useful beggin' or thievin'? Rich folks are there for us to steal from. I've spent enough time teaching you how to screw a penny out of a mug's pocket. You're twelve now, so you should be bringin' in money of yer own. A skinny, sickly-looking girl like you will fetch plenty from beggin'. If you just let your hair get knotted once in a while… Stop brushing it for gawd's sake! And try hobblin' a bit. There's plenty to be earned for a beggar with a limp. And a cough. Why don't you try coughin' a little—'

'I ain't beggin' or stealin' no more,' Lizzie interrupted him sharply. 'It ain't no life.'

She wasn't going to pretend to have a cough for anyone. Ma died from a cough last year. Grief pinched at Lizzie's heart as she remembered her mother spitting up blood, half-delirious with fever. Lizzie had pleaded with Pa, 'Let me stay home and tend to her.' But Pa had dragged her onto the streets, making use of her tear-stained face to squeeze money from tender-hearted passers-by.

Lizzie had known that Pa had a half-crown in his pocket on that day, but he wouldn't spend it on a doctor for Ma – he was saving it for the gin palace. Ma had to cough and sweat alone, without even a sip of brandy to ease her suffering.

At least I was with her at the end. Lizzie closed her eyes, remembering how soft Ma's hair had felt as she'd stroked it. Tears pricked in her eyes as the memories filled her mind, but she blinked them away – she wasn't going to let Pa see her cry. Like Ma said when her older brother John had died three years ago: 'You can waste the day cryin', or you can tuck him safe in your heart and let his memory keep you warm.'

Lizzie shoved the memory away. She couldn't bring John back. Or Ma. But they were both safe in her heart.

Pa's boots scraped the floor. 'What do you mean, you ain't beggin' or stealin' no more?'

Lizzie heard a ripping noise. She looked up with a gasp. Her father was clutching a handful of paper streamers.

'No!' She leaped and grabbed his arm. But it was too late – he'd torn them and flung them onto the floor.

'My flower paper!' Lizzie dropped to her knees and began snatching it up frantically. 'I was going to earn enough to get out of here.'

'Get out of 'ere?' With a heavy boot, Pa began to grind the paper into the grime. 'Why do you want to get out of 'ere? Are you too good for the Castle, mi'lady?'

'I'm done with stealin' and beggin'!' Lizzie jumped to her feet. 'I wish *you* were too!' Trembling with rage, she grabbed the jar off the table and splashed vinegar over Pa. The soap bubbled and frothed on his legs till they looked leprous with ulcers. 'That's what you wanted, ain't it?' she shrieked. She'd seen him use the soap and vinegar trick a hundred times. Fake sores earned more pennies to spend at the gin palace. 'With legs like that, you'll earn enough to drink yourself silly!'

Pa growled, and Lizzie swallowed, scared. What had she done? Pa's shins were dripping with froth, and fear dropped like a stone into the pit of her belly as his face hardened into a scowl. She knew what he could do; she'd watched him beat Ma and John enough times.

He lunged at her. 'You ungrateful guttersnipe!'

Lizzie ducked.

'I'll murder you!' he roared.

Before she could duck again, his fist slammed against her cheek. It sent her reeling backwards, and she knocked against the wall, making plates rattle on the shelves.

Half-blind with pain, she saw Pa coming at her again, his face dark with fury. Terror flared through her and she dived between his legs and darted for the door. Fingers tugged at her skirt, but Lizzie tore free and raced out into the hall.

Swinging round the banister post she ran down the stairs, taking them three at a time. Her father's boots thundered after her, but she didn't look round before bursting out into the street.

People jostled along the narrow lane, and she slipped between them, bobbing and weaving, nimble as a prize-fighter, till Pa's roars faded far behind her.

Heart thumping, she stumbled to a halt and leaned against a wall. People passed, hardly seeing her, no one looking twice at her flushed face. Rat's Castle was filled with street urchins – for all anyone knew, Lizzie was just another pickpocket fleeing a copper.

She loosened her shawl, hot from running. Thank heaven it'd been a freezing night. The hard April frost meant she'd gone to her bed wearing every piece of clothing she possessed. If it had been summer, she'd be in her nightgown.

She looked about, wondering which way to go. A man was herding a pig along the muddy lane. Two washerwomen heaved sacks of clothing on their backs, bent under their weight, while a rosy-cheeked fellow balanced a tray in the crook of his arm. 'Hot sheeps' feet!' he called.

The delicious smell made Lizzie's mouth water, but her pockets were empty. She glanced down the lane, terrified that she would see her father's face.

'Lizzie?' A wizened hand grasped her sleeve. 'Spare some change?'

Lizzie pulled away, recognizing one of the old crones who begged outside their tenement. 'I've got nothing.'

'Is that Lizzie Brown?' A blind old man was tapping his way toward her with a cane.

She had to hide – this pair would sell her back to Pa for a penny. She hopped over the gutter and ducked between the washerwomen's bulging sacks. Keeping low, she shadowed them this way and that as they wended their way through the alleys of Rat's Castle. She passed closed doors, boarded windows and narrow passageways. Above her the sky was no more than a strip of blue between the crowded roofs.

Where could she hide? She hadn't got a penny on her, and she would need one for an inn or a room. Thanks to her father, she knew how to snatch watches or handkerchiefs, but she was determined no one would make a pickpocket of her. Mud splashed her boots as she followed the chattering washerwomen. One of them glanced back, frowning suspiciously.

'Oi, what you followin' us for?'

'I wasn't followin'!'

'Gerr-away!'

As the washerwoman lifted a hand to clip her ear, Lizzie darted down an alley. Hardly wide enough to squeeze through, it ran between ramshackle houses. Light glowed at the end. Her heart lifting, Lizzie hurried along and burst out into sunshine.

She blinked in the brightness. Hansom cabs whisked by, their wheels rattling. Men in stiff collars, bedecked with glittering watch chains, strode down wide, clean pavements. Women in stripes and ruffles twirled parasols as they passed gleaming shop windows.

Oxford Street.

After the filth and gloom of Rat's Castle, it was like stepping into another world.

CHAPTER 2

She'd escaped!

Lizzie's heart soared as she stared at the bright, busy street, then a sharp knock on the ankles sent her staggering.

'Move out of the way.' The well-dressed gentleman hardly looked at her as he swept her aside with his silver-topped cane and marched past.

Lizzie heard a rattling noise beside her. She looked and saw pennies in a cup. A beggar, ragged and stinking, stood a footstep away, chin lifted proudly, a sign hanging limply around his neck:

Crippled in Crimea

As he lifted his tin cup apologetically, a woman in a feathered hat slowed and opened her purse. She dropped a coin into the beggar's cup, then held another out to Lizzie.

'No! No, ma'am!' Lizzie backed away in horror. 'I ain't askin' for your money.' She turned and ran. As faces blurred around her, she pictured Pa grinning.

See, I told you so! he chuckled. *You're a beggar like me and you'll never be anything more.*

'That's not true!' Lizzie sobbed. She didn't care if anyone heard her.

'Ee-ee-eels, alive-o!'

She tore past a man with a barrel strapped to his back. Eels slapped and sloshed inside. Lizzie clenched her fists. 'I'll find work. I know I will!'

But how?

Blinded by tears, she raced along the gutter till the world suddenly opened around her. The smart buildings gave way to wide lawns.

Lizzie stumbled to a halt. Trees lined the far horizon. Birds swooped between their shimmering branches and sunshine glittered on water in the distance.

The surprise of green grass and blue sky calmed her panic. She had never even *imagined* anywhere this beautiful. *I found this all by myself!* Lizzie caught her breath. *And I'll find a new life too.*

Tilting her chin up, she marched toward the wrought-iron gates, where the road swept in among the lawns. People streamed around her, chattering excitedly. A woman in a feathered hat pushed ahead of her, pulling a smartly dressed girl by the hand.

'What is this place?' Lizzie called to the girl.

'Hyde Park.' The girl held onto her hat as a gang of boys jostled past.

'Where's everyone going?' The crowd was swarming through the gates, eager as folks hurrying to a music hall.

'Don't you know?' the girl cried, but the woman in the feathered hat jerked her away.

'Read all about it!' A paperboy waved a newspaper above his head. 'The Phantom strikes again!'

'The Phantom?' A young woman in a bright red dress snatched the paper from the boy's hand.

'Oi!' The boy held out his hand. 'A penny, if you please.'

'Here.' The woman fumbled in her purse, one

eye on her paper.

The boy took her coin, tugged another paper from a bundle tucked under his arm and flapped it in the air. 'Rozzers dumbfounded as Phantom gives them the slip!'

The Phantom? Lizzie craned to see.

A man in a trilby was holding the woman in red's arm. 'What's 'e done this time, Gladys?'

'Another burglary.' Gladys pressed closer to the man. 'Oh, Ernest! That's the fourth burglary this month and no one's even found a footprint.'

'Slyest burglar in London's 'istory!' The paperboy pushed himself forward and began offering papers left and right. 'No one knows how he gets in.'

'Or out,' Earnest muttered.

'He must be a ghost,' Gladys gasped. 'It says here that he got through three locked doors and broke into an uncrackable safe this time.'

Lizzie stood on tiptoes and peeked at Gladys's paper:

PHANTOM TARGETS LOWNDES SQUARE IN DARING JEWEL THEFT

She swiftly skimmed the article below, picking out the words she could read, just as Ma had taught her.

Robbery while the family slept... No sign of a break-in... Famous psychic, Mrs Palfry, claims she saw him in a dream ... described his features to an artist. Below the words was a sketch of the cruellest face Lizzie had ever seen. A chill ran through her.

Ernest whistled through his teeth. 'That's no human face.'

'Perhaps it's a mask,' Gladys suggested.

'I hope so.' Ernest tucked his arm protectively round her narrow waist.

Music sounded suddenly outside the park gates. As Lizzie turned round, the crowd parted and she glimpsed a man in a red spangled jacket. Behind him, a riot of noise and colour filled the road.

A parade!

Lizzie scurried to the side of the road and pressed in among the crowd, her eyes wide as a huge grey animal lumbered past. She'd only ever seen them in pictures before: an elephant, a real one! It was huge, with a big round belly and a long, dangling trunk. It was draped in colourful silk and crowned with a seat as ornate as any carriage. A lady, fat as a Christmas pudding, waved from the top.

'Roll up!' The man in the spangled jacket was waving

a long, golden baton. 'Roll up! For Fitzy's Travelling Circus. Watch death-defying stunts! Marvel at acrobatic feats never seen before. See Sullivans' Bareback Balleta. Be amazed by Anita, the World's Smallest Woman. Mermaids, camels, elephants and lions – Fitzy's Circus has got it all!'

More elephants lumbered past, followed by the band. A big bass drum bounced on the belly of a fat man. Cymbals flashed in the sunshine, and trumpets blasted in time to the beat. Then came six golden horses, their riders glittering in matching jackets.

Lizzie stared up at them, mouth open. One was a girl about her own age with flaming red hair that streamed down her back. What must it feel like to be up there on horseback? The girl suddenly caught Lizzie's eye. She grinned, then threw her feet skyward and balanced on her saddle in a graceful handstand. Lizzie clapped wildly.

'Look, Ma!' A young boy squeezed past Lizzie and pointed at the carriage, which rumbled behind the riders.

Lizzie dragged her gaze from the girl on horseback. Through the iron bars of the carriage, she could see a light brown animal pacing. It was making a loud snarling noise and its tail swished menacingly. A sign above the cage read 'King Of The Jungle'.

'Alfred, you get back here!' A woman grabbed the boy's hand and tugged him away.

Lizzie stood, rooted to the spot, as the dazzling parade flowed past. Acrobats balanced on each other's shoulders. Clowns tumbled and teased the crowd, squirting water from flowers and pulling pennies from children's ears. She clasped her hands against her heart. Surely she could find some work here? There were animals to be fed and cleaned out, costumes to be laundered. Her mind whirled with possibilities as she watched the circus disappear into the park.

Kids were dodging through the crowd, handing out flyers:

'First show at dusk!'

'Bring the family! Threepenny a ticket. Five tickets for a shilling!'

Lizzie hardly heard them. She was following the trail of muck and rutted earth the circus had left in its wake.

By the time she caught up, the carriages were parked. The dazzling showmen were leaping down from their boxes and stripping off their fancy jackets. As Lizzie watched, a dozen burly men, sleeves rolled up, heaved a huge bundle of red and black striped canvas from the back of a cart. Shouting back and forth to one another, they began to unfold it, and before long, they were winching the round pointed roof of a circus tent into the bright blue sky.

'Hey, Joss! Pass a mallet!' A curly-headed man heaved a thick guy rope and hooked the end around a loose wooden peg. His muscles strained at the effort as he held it in place.

Quickly, Lizzie scanned the grass. A mallet was lying just a few feet away. She raced to it and dragged it across the grass. 'Here!'

The curly-headed man glanced quickly over his shoulder. 'Knock this peg in before this rope pulls it back out, love.'

Lizzie heaved the mallet as high as she could and let it drop onto the peg. The peg sank deep into the soft earth.

'Thanks.' The man let go of the rope and rubbed the sweat from his brow. Then he frowned at Lizzie. 'Who are you?'

'I'm Lizzie Brown.' She looked at him hopefully. 'Is there anything else I can do?'

'You can stay out the way.' The man waved her away.

'The tent's not safe till every peg's driven in.'

'I'll be careful,' Lizzie promised.

'Girls ain't no good for heavy work.' The man strode away, not looking back.

Lizzie stuck out her tongue. 'I hammered in your peg for you, didn't I?' She glanced around and spotted a woman struggling to drape a striped canvas over a wooden booth. 'Let me help.' She grabbed a corner of the woman's tent and began pulling it.

'Gerroff!' the woman snapped. 'You'll tear it, you lummox!'

Lizzie let go. 'I was only tryin' to help.'

'Go help somewhere else.' The woman turned her back.

Lizzie's heart sank. Wasn't there anything she could do? Around her, the site rang with hammering and cursing. Sideshows began to dot the field around the big tent and, beyond them, Lizzie could see the great frames of the swing-boats and roundabouts silhouetted against the horizon. Perhaps once everything was set up, she'd be able to find some way to earn her supper. She wandered to the edge of the field and sank into the grass.

The sun was warm now and the low beech hedge

behind shielded her from the breeze. Lizzie watched the circus grow, studying faces and voices, trying to guess where the most work was and who'd be most likely to give it to her. A woman sat sewing up a tear in a wide sheet of canvas. Another was building a fire in front of her stall. There had to be some way to win their trust, but right now Lizzie couldn't think of one.

The sun slid across the sky until she felt her eyelids droop. Exhausted, she let her thoughts drift and, within minutes, she was dozing, and dreaming.

The alleys and doorways of Rat's Castle twisted and snaked at the edge of her dreams. Her breath quickened as she saw eyes flashing from the shadows. She pelted forward into darkness and ran blind.

Suddenly the Phantom loomed ahead of her. His grotesque face grinned a whisker from hers, a smile twisting his lips…

Lizzie opened her eyes with a start. The nightmare had been so vivid she had to keep blinking, to make sure the face wasn't really there. She shook her head to chase away the terrifying image. Nightmares were nothing new to Lizzie. She'd always had vivid dreams, and when she was little she'd loved to tell her mother about them when she woke up. But since Ma had died her dreams had become darker, and even more realistic.

It was dark and crowds were swarming toward the circus. Music thrummed from the big striped tent. Stallholders hollered beside their booths. The swing-boat swooped up and down against the night-black sky, squeals of terror exploding with each drop of the gondola.

'You'll catch cold on that damp grass.'

Lizzie looked up at the sound of a voice. An old man with a kind smile was standing over her.

'I'm fine.' She scrambled to her feet.

'Here.' He held out a tin mug, brimming with hot soup. 'This'll keep the chill off.'

She stared at the soup warily. The man was dressed like a toff but his voice had the twang of Rat's Castle. Lizzie said, 'What do you want for it? I ain't got no money.'

The man pressed the mug gently into her hands. 'Just give the cup back to the soup-seller when you're done.' He nodded toward a small canvas booth set up nearby, where a woman, sleeves rolled, stirred a large iron pot as it hung over a fire.

Lizzie narrowed her eyes. What if he was one of those do-gooders? He might make her go home to Pa.

Or to an orphanage. Or to the workhouse. But the soup smelled good and her belly was rumbling. She leaned over it and let the steam warm her face.

'Here.' He slid a penny into her palm. 'Treat yourself.'

Lizzie backed away. 'I ain't a beggar, sir.'

'I know.' The man gazed at her steadily. 'I was poor and hungry when I was your age, so I know what it feels like.'

Lizzie watched him walk away. The hot mug stung her hands and the soup burned her lips but she swallowed anyway. She was so hungry it was worth the scalding.

She felt warmer by the time she'd finished. The lights from the circus flickered enticingly. Shaking the dampness from her skirt, she crossed the grass. 'Thanks, missus.' She offered the mug to the soup-seller as she reached her iron pot.

The woman took it without looking up. 'Better hurry, dearie. Next show is the last show.'

Lizzie hadn't realized it was so late. Had she really slept so long? She hurried among the booths, peeking past the canvas doorways held tantalizingly aside by their owners.

'Walk in! Walk in!' A stallholder brandished an ivory cane. 'Come and see the Pig-Faced Woman!' Lizzie strained to see into the shadowy tent. Above the door a painted sign showed a picture of a woman dressed in a crinoline. Lace cuffs framed pretty hands but, above the collar, the woman had a snout, beady eyes and pointy ears that poked out from under her hair.

'Come on, dearie,' the stallholder enticed. 'Just a penny to see one of the Wonders of the World.'

Lizzie clutched her penny in her palm.

'See the world's only captive mermaid!' another stallholder hollered. 'Come inside and watch her comb her golden hair while she flaps her fishy tail.'

Lizzie glanced from the Mermaid to the Pig-Faced Woman. She only had one penny. Which one should she choose?

Then another sign caught her eye:

Ten in One

'I spy a curious young lady.' A showman twirled the waxed tips of his moustache between his fingers. 'Come closer, my dear. Come and see ten amazing acts for just one penny!'

Ten amazing acts.

Without hesitating, Lizzie headed straight for his tent, handed over her penny and ducked inside.

Visitors clustered in front of small stages, their astonished faces glowing in the gaslight. Eagerly, Lizzie wriggled her way into the nearest crowd. As she popped out at the front, she saw a man standing bare-chested beside a smouldering brazier. With a flourish, he lit a long taper on the burning coals and lowered the flame into his mouth.

Lizzie gasped as he closed his lips around it. He stared at her with sparkling eyes, then opened his mouth to let out a cloud of steam. Where was the flame? Lizzie watched in awe as he relit his taper, opened his mouth and extinguished it again as easily as snuffing a candle.

What other wonders were waiting for her to see? Lizzie pushed her way to the next stage where a miniature rocking chair creaked in front of a small fireplace. A tiny hearth-rug covered the stage and little curtains dressed tiny windows painted on the backdrop. It looked like a parlour built for a child, and the woman seated in the rocking chair was not much bigger than a doll. She rocked back and forth in her chair, sucking on a clay pipe and reading a newspaper on her knee. Above the stage, the sign read:

Anita, the World's Smallest Woman

Lizzie struggled to get a better look, but the crowds were too thick. Then, to her amazement, Anita noticed her and waved. 'Let the little one through to the front please, ladies and gents!' she called. 'She's paid her penny, same as you.'

People laughed and shuffled aside to let her through.

Lizzie beamed up at Anita. 'You're real!' she said.

'Well, I ain't made of wood, if that's what you were wonderin'.' Anita winked.

A gasp burst from the crowd beside her. Lizzie turned and saw on the next stage a wizened old man dressed in nothing but a loincloth. With a serene smile, he hopped from one foot to the other on a pile of glass shards. *His feet must be shredded*, she thought. But the glass shards sparkled clear as fresh water with no sign of blood.

A showman strutted at the front of the stage. 'I discovered this ancient fakir in the mountains of Persia. Each morning he bathes in Epsom salts, and each night he drinks a potion of Eastern herbs which makes his skin as tough as leather.'

Lizzie stared at the old man's skin that did indeed seem as brown and weather-beaten as a cobbler's apron.

She turned, breathless with amazement, and saw a tall woman, black as ebony and tall as a giant. The sign above her read: *The Amazon Queen*.

Then a blade flashed at the corner of Lizzie's eye. On the next stage, a man was tilting his head back and sliding a sword down his throat until the hilt rested on his lips.

Lizzie's eyes widened. In the circus, anything could happen. Surely there could be some small place here for her?

CHAPTER 3

Silk rustled behind her and Lizzie whirled round.

A smiling woman – hefty as a dray-horse, and done up in brightly coloured ruffles – began to chivvy her toward the exit.

'But I only just got in!' Lizzie objected. 'I've not seen it all.'

'Then come back tomorra.' The other visitors were streaming out already. 'Why don't you pop along to the big tent? The last performance'll be starting any moment. We're closing up here. Poor Anita is worn to a shred.'

'You're not wrong, Flora.' In her miniature parlour,

Anita slid forward in her tiny chair. 'I feel tattered as a snippet.' She began rubbing her feet with small, plump hands. 'Lawks!' she huffed. 'I've lost all feeling in my toes.' She hopped to the ground and began to limp toward her pint-sized fireplace.

In the tall booth opposite, the Amazon Queen pulled off her feather-and-bone headdress and dusted down her skirt. She called to Anita. 'Come for your tommy tucker at my wagon, 'Nita. Oi'm makin' stew.'

Lizzie stared in surprise. The Amazon Queen – twice as tall as Lizzie and as exotic as a bird of paradise – spoke with the raucous East End accent of a music-hall singer. 'I thought she was from Africa!'

'She is.' Flora folded her hands on her belly and leaned back proudly. 'I taught her English myself. Quick learner, she was.'

The Amazon Queen gave a throaty laugh. 'In Africa I speak like a queen. In England I speak like a washerwoman.'

'What do you mean?' Flora threw up her arms. 'Queen Victoria herself don't speak no better than me.'

The Amazon Queen ignored her and nodded regally to the fakir, then the sword swallower. 'Why don't the pair of you join us too? And if you'd be so kind as to bring a lil' summit to throw in the pot, we can turn me plucked pigeon into a proper fricassee.'

Lizzie felt a nudge from behind. It was Flora again. 'You still 'ere, little 'un? Go find your ma. She'll be missin' you.' Flora shooed her out with the rest of the visitors, and before she could argue, Lizzie found herself outside in the dusky evening.

She shivered. Purple clouds streaked a pink sky. An evening chill was flooding Hyde Park. She lifted her wool skirt, pulling it tight around her shoulders like a shawl and leaving her tattered petticoats to flutter around her legs.

The crowds were thinning as the last of the sideshow visitors filtered into the big tent. A top-hatted man in a patchwork waistcoat beckoned latecomers through the brightly lit entrance. 'Last Show! Last Show!' He swapped their threepenny-bits for tickets and waved them inside where flickering lights swallowed them.

Lizzie's shoulders drooped. Her purse was as empty as her belly. Heart heavy, she wandered across the grass while figures worked around her, closing up sideshows and lighting lamps outside caravans. Canvas flapped in the breeze, while music swelled inside the big tent, and she could hear the crowd murmuring with anticipation.

The show was about to begin.

The bruise on Lizzie's cheek ached as the cold jabbed at it. Pa would give her another if she went home.

A happy roar rose from the show tent. The sound of it swirled around Lizzie and she stopped beside a flower bed, thick with bushes, and stared back across the field. This would be a safe place to rest. She sank to the ground and crawled beneath one of the bushes. Curling up tight as a hedgehog, she listened to the ringmaster calling out the first act as stones grated against her bony arms. Music thumped and the crowd cheered with delight while Lizzie snuggled deeper into her petticoats, trying to escape the cold and imagining what was happening inside the warmth of the circus tent.

As the night drew on, Lizzie carried on sitting there – long after the show had finished and the audience had gone home. An owl screeched overhead and made her gasp as, aching all over, she crept out from beneath the bush into a sleeping world. The big tent flapped eerily in the darkness and here and there caravan windows showed lights, but no one stirred. The owl screeched again and Lizzie's teeth began to chatter. She had to find somewhere warmer.

Quiet as a mouse, she crept between the tents and caravans. A horse stamped beside her, making her jump. Warmth pulsed from its flanks. Heavy-hooved and clumsy with sleep, it knocked against her. Lizzie backed away past a caravan and glanced up at its door. Light flooded from a small pane of glass, as laughter sounded inside and Lizzie could smell the mouth-watering scent of food. She wondered if the Amazon Queen was inside, eating fricassee with the World's Smallest Woman.

The horse whinnied and thrust its head toward her inquisitively. Lizzie darted backward, slipping into the shadows beside the big tent. She followed the striped canvas, away from the booths and caravans. Here in the quiet moonlight, she saw pens with animals shifting about between makeshift wooden fences. They huffed and sighed, breathing softly with sleep.

Lizzie leaned over a fence. A small herd of ponies were bunched together, their coats golden in the moonlight as they dozed. In the pen beside them, two huge beasts paced the grass. Lizzie stared at their long gangly legs. Then she saw the huge humps on their backs. 'Blimey!' she whispered. 'God must've been havin' a laugh when he made you.' The creatures paused and gazed at her with huge, dark eyes, their wide nostrils twitching. Then they carried on pacing, their broad, soft feet silent on the grass.

A breeze lifted Lizzie's hair and made her shiver. Spotting a gap between the pens, she squeezed into it, eager to be out of the biting wind. She felt hay beneath her feet and sank gratefully into it. In the pen beside her, the two strange creatures tucked their legs clumsily beneath them and settled down for the night, and Lizzie could feel their warmth through the slats of the fence. Wriggling closer, she closed her eyes and rested, relaxing to the sound of their soft breathing.

'Hey!'

A stick jabbed her ribs.

Lizzie sat up with a jolt. Her first thought was: *Pa's going to hit me again.*

Two feet stood beside her. One foot was small; the other was large and misshapen. She looked up with a gasp and saw a face frowning down.

The stick jabbed her again. It wasn't Pa, but Lizzie's heart was still pounding. She pushed the stick away.

'Gerroff!' She leaped to her feet. 'Stop it!' She found herself staring into the eyes of a skinny boy, smaller than she was. 'There's no need to keep poking me,' she mumbled.

The boy glared at her. 'You shouldn't be here.'

'I was just leaving anyway.' Dawn was lighting the sky behind the big tent. She stepped forward. 'Let me past.'

'What's going on here?' A man sauntered up behind the scowling boy and looked Lizzie up and down. She recognized the man from the big tent. He was still wearing his patchwork waistcoat and top hat. 'What have you found, Mally?'

'She was sleeping in the hay,' the boy answered without taking his eyes off Lizzie.

'We don't want that, do we, Malachy, m'boy?' The man's eyes twinkled. 'If we feed the animals girl-flavoured hay they might develop a taste for young 'uns.'

Lizzie glanced anxiously at the strange animals in the pen beside her. 'They wouldn't eat me, would they?' she gasped.

Malachy laughed. 'They eat hay, not girls.'

The man rested his hand on Malachy's shoulder.

'I reckon a lion might enjoy her.' He tipped his head to one side. 'Though there's not much meat on her.'

Lizzie backed away. 'I-I'm sorry I slept here, but I…'

'Now, now, little 'un.' The man nudged the brim of his hat so it sat back on his head. 'We don't mean any harm.'

Malachy shifted his lumpen foot. 'Sorry I poked you so hard.' He lifted his walking stick apologetically. Now he'd stopped glaring, his thin face looked more mischievous than unkind. 'I thought you were a stray dog.' He reached over the fence and patted one of the strange animals. 'Dogs worry the animals.'

Lizzie looked down at her shabby grey dress with dismay. 'You thought I was a stray dog?'

Malachy flushed. 'Sorry.'

The man straightened his hat and smiled. 'I'm Edward Fitzgerald. Most people call me Fitzy. And this is my son, Malachy.'

Lizzie stuck out her hand. 'I'm Lizzie.'

'Pleased to meet you, Lizzie.' Mr Fitzgerald reached past Malachy and shook Lizzie's hand. 'What are you doing here? Are you lost?'

'No.' Lizzie lifted her chin. 'I'm looking for work.'

Mr Fitzgerald rubbed his chin. 'You look a bit

skinny to be any good for hard work.'

'I've worked since I was seven years old,' Lizzie retorted.

Malachy looked at his dad. 'Why don't we give her a try?' he suggested. 'You were saying just this morning there's more work than hands round here.'

'Workers cost money.' Mr Fitzgerald frowned.

'I don't need much,' Lizzie told him quickly. 'And I'll tell you what – I'll work for a whole week for you without takin' a penny, just for food. If you don't think I'm worth it by then, I'll go away quiet.'

Mr Fitzgerald looked her up and down again. 'I don't know about that.'

'I'm a hard worker,' Lizzie urged.

'Go on, Pop,' Malachy chimed.

Mr Fitzgerald scratched his head. 'All right, then. I'll give you a trial.'

'You won't be sorry!' Lizzie wanted to hug him.

'You can't sleep here, though,' Fitzy went on.

Lizzie glanced at the sky. 'It's nearly dawn,' she pointed out. 'I don't need more sleep. I can start work now if you like.' She wanted to prove she was strong and willing.

'Breakfast first.' Mr Fitzgerald headed away. 'Take

40

her to Ma Sullivan, Mally,' he called over his shoulder before ducking down and disappearing under the canvas wall of the big tent.

'Follow me.' Malachy began to walk toward the caravans. His curly hair was cropped close to his head and his body was wiry beneath his shirt and breeches. If it wasn't for the heavy boot on his misshapen foot, Lizzie could believe he was a changeling child left by pixies. He moved fast and she had to run to keep up, swerving around guy ropes and jumping over tent pegs as she went.

The circus was already awake. A caravan door opened as they passed and a clown peered out.

'I thought everyone'd sleep late,' Lizzie called after Malachy. 'They must have worked till near midnight.'

'Dawn's the best chance the performers get to practise,' Malachy answered. 'No passers-by gawking.'

Two burly men with rolled-up sleeves crossed Lizzie's path and she stopped to let them by. One of them carried a heavy coil of rope, slung across his chest. The other was wheeling a penny-farthing bicycle. An elegant young woman wrapped in a brightly embroidered shawl glided behind them, and Lizzie gasped as she passed.

Malachy stopped and span round. 'What's the matter?'

Lizzie pointed at the young woman. 'She's got no clothes on!' Beneath the shawl she could see the young woman's legs clad in nothing but spangled tights. 'Where are her petticoats?'

'That's her costume.' Malachy laughed. 'She can't practise in petticoats.'

'Practise what?'

'She rides the penny farthing on the high wire.'

Lizzie gasped. 'Not really!'

Malachy grinned. 'Her act is near the beginning of the show.' He pointed to a group of wiry youths turning somersaults and Lizzie recognized the acrobats from the parade. 'They usually come after her,' Malachy told her. He pointed past a wagon loaded with straw. A boy was cantering in a circle on one of the golden ponies. As Lizzie watched, the boy leaped up and balanced on his hands on the back of the prancing pony, just like the red-haired girl from the parade.

'Lordy!' Lizzie stared in wonder. 'Does everyone here have an act?'

Malachy tapped his clumpy foot with his stick. 'Everyone except me.'

Lizzie glanced down, wondering what to say.

'Don't worry.' Malachy shrugged. 'I got extra brains instead.'

'But—'

Before Lizzie could speak, Malachy grabbed her arm and tugged her sideways. 'Always keep your eyes peeled around here.' He pointed to one of the elephants swaying heavily toward them. 'If you get trampled it's your own fault.'

'It's huge!' Lizzie's heart lurched as it tramped so close that she felt the air stir around her. Its ears flapped like wings and its wrinkly flesh rippled with each thumping step. She gripped onto Malachy as the ground shook beneath her feet. 'Does it trample many folk?'

Malachy laughed. 'Only people daft enough not to see her coming.'

A tiny Indian man followed. He wore a vest and wide braces and carried a broom in one hand and a cake of soap in the other. 'Good morning, Malachy,' he called.

'Morning, Zezete.' Malachy then patted the elephant. 'Morning, Akula.' The animal lifted its trunk and trumpeted loudly.

Lizzie covered her ears. Then her nose. The stench

following the animal made her eyes water.

'Akula's going for her bath.' Malachy shielded his eyes. Sunshine was sparkling on the Serpentine. 'I hope the park keepers aren't awake yet. I don't know if they'd approve of her bathing in their pond.'

Lizzie giggled. 'Can we watch?'

'Don't be rude!' Malachy grinned. 'Poor Akula's shy about bath time. She worries about her weight.'

As his eyes flashed teasingly, Lizzie felt a jab of grief – that was the sort of silly thing her brother John would have said. She pushed the thought away and asked, 'Ain't they dangerous, with those big twisty teeth?'

'No,' said Malachy. 'They may be big but they're gentle as anything. Not like the lion.' He pointed towards the wagon with iron bars that Lizzie had seen on the parade. 'That's Leo's cage,' he told her. 'He's our lion.'

'Why's it empty?' Lizzie glanced nervously over her shoulder.

Malachy leaned close. 'He escaped last night,' he whispered. 'We've been looking for him ever since.' Without waiting for a response, he crossed the grass and stopped outside a bright yellow caravan. 'Nora! Erin!' he called up the ladder steps.

A curly redhead poked out of the door. 'What?'

'Come and meet Lizzie.'

The head ducked back inside. 'Nora!'

'The Sullivans are the best bareback riders in Europe,' Malachy told Lizzie as she caught up. 'That was Conor you saw practising on the pony.'

Lizzie heard the door open again and two girls, rosy-cheeked and both with thick red curly hair, stepped out of the caravan.

'Hello,' said the first girl with a smile. 'I'm Nora.'

'And I'm Erin.' Her identical twin sister pushed ahead and grabbed Lizzie's hand. 'Pleased to meet you.' She shook it enthusiastically.

'Excuse me!' Nora elbowed Erin aside. 'Forgive my sister.' Her blue eyes twinkled as she spoke. 'She's an awful hoyden.'

'I am not,' Erin objected.

'You are so.' Nora put her hands on her hips and faced Erin squarely.

Malachy slid in between them. 'Before you start brawling, I was hoping your ma could find a bit of breakfast for Lizzie.'

'Is she staying?' Nora asked.

'Is she joining the circus?' Erin chimed in. Their

squabble forgotten, they both turned on Lizzie, faces eager for answers. 'What's your act?' Erin asked.

'High wire,' Nora guessed, through half-closed eyes.

'No, no,' Erin butted in. 'She's not got enough flesh on her.' She squeezed the muscles on Lizzie's arm.

Lizzie pulled away. 'I-I don't have an act.'

'Not yet,' Nora said. 'But Fitzy will find you a speciality before long.'

Erin laughed. 'Even if it's just balancing on Akula's trunk!'

Nora nodded. 'She could do that. She looks light as a feather.'

'What is going on out here?'

Lizzie looked up the caravan steps as a ruddy-cheeked woman appeared, hands on hips, in the doorway. Strands of dark hair whisked around her face, which was handsome and lit by flashing blue eyes.

Nora raced toward the woman and reached up the caravan steps to tug on the hem of her skirts. 'Can Lizzie have breakfast with us, Ma? Fitzy just hired her.'

Lizzie looked shyly up at Nora's mother. 'If you've not got nothin' to spare, I'll be fine,' she lied. Her belly was growling.

'There's always a bit to spare in the Sullivan family.'

Ma Sullivan looked over her shoulder. 'Budge up, Patrick. Sean, make some space. There's going to be an extra kiddie at the table.'

Before she knew what was happening, Lizzie felt Erin and Nora bundling her up the caravan stairs. Inside, the walls were lined with cupboards and shelves. A stove was squeezed in the corner beside the door and in the middle was a table. Two dark-haired boys, with lean, muscular arms were wrestling across the top of it, while a man sucked on a pipe, half-hidden by a newspaper at the far end.

'Patrick, Sean, behave yourselves,' Ma ordered.

Grumbling, the two boys slid back into their seats.

'Those are two of my brothers,' Erin sniffed. 'And that's Pa.'

Pa lifted his pipe. 'Welcome to the Sullivan Palace,' he called and went back to his paper.

'Ma opens up the tea tent after ten in the morning,' said Nora. 'If you work at Fitzy's, you can go there for a meal or a brew any time.'

One of the boys reached out and ruffled Erin's hair fondly. 'Don't tell me you've brought home another stray puppy.' He winked at Lizzie.

Erin ducked away. 'Patrick Sullivan, don't be

rude to our guest!'

'Lizzie's come for breakfast,' Nora added, flashing a challenging stare at Sean. 'So no playing any of your pranks on her.'

Sean held up his hands. 'It's Brendan and Conor you need to be warning.'

Nora shook her hair from her face. 'And so I will when they get back from practice.'

Ma Sullivan pushed her way to the stove and pulled a pot from the hob. 'I hope you like porridge, Lizzie.'

Lizzie's stomach growled in reply.

'I think that's a yes,' Pa grunted from behind his paper.

After breakfast, Lizzie plumped down in the grass and leaned against the tall, spoked wheel of the caravan. She felt sleepy, her belly full, the sun warm on her face.

Nora settled beside her. 'Ma wants you to stay with us. She won't have any child sleep out when we can make room.'

'Are you sure?' Lizzie wondered how the six Sullivan children and Ma and Pa managed to sleep in that small caravan as it was.

'Look.' Nora wriggled between the wheels and opened a door to a wide square compartment underneath the caravan.

Lizzie's eyes widened. 'We don't have to sleep in there, do we?'

Nora spluttered with laughter. 'No, silly! We pack all the costumes and knick-knacks here in the bellybox. Then there's room to make up the bunk beds. You can squeeze between Erin and me. We'll be as snug as bedbugs.'

The caravan creaked as Pa settled himself on the steps and carried on reading his newspaper.

Lizzie lay back in the grass and closed her eyes. She'd be warm tonight and surrounded by new friends. Smiling, she listened to the sounds of the circus. Horses whinnied, Akula trumpeted, and somewhere there was a snarling noise.

Lizzie sat up with a jerk. 'Lion!'

'What's the matter, Lizzie?' Erin leaped down past Pa.

Nora leaned close. 'You look like you've seen a ghost!'

'The lion!' Lizzie jumped to her feet and stared

around, heart racing. Was that a flash of golden mane behind the feed wagon? 'The escaped lion!'

'What escaped lion?' Nora was staring at her as though she were mad.

'Leo! His cage was empty! Malachy said he'd escaped!'

'Escaped?' Pa slapped his thigh, laughing. 'Leo's too old to escape, and if he did he's not got teeth, nor sense enough to harm a lamb. Malachy's been pulling your leg—' Pa Sullivan broke off suddenly, his attention fixed on his paper. 'Lord preserve us!' He jabbed the paper with his finger. 'He's held a candle to the Devil this time.'

'Who has?' Erin raced to his side.

'The Phantom,' Pa said.

The Phantom? Lizzie forgot the lion at once.

'Did you say the Phantom?' Patrick appeared at the caravan door, eyes bright. 'Has he cracked another safe?' he said, grinning.

'Patrick Sullivan!' Erin frowned at her brother. 'Safe-cracking is not a sport, y'know! The Phantom's a wicked burglar and he's going straight to Hell when they catch him.'

'Let's hope they catch him soon,' Pa Sullivan said grimly.

'Why?' Erin peered at her father's paper. 'What's he done this time?'

'He's turned nasty, that's what,' Pa growled. 'Some poor fella in Spitalfields went blundering in on him while he was robbing a house. Got bashed over the head for his trouble and left for dead.'

Erin grasped Pa's arm. 'Did the Phantom kill him?'

'Close enough,' Pa muttered.

Nora squeezed closer to Lizzie. 'Why do folks say he's a ghost, Pa?' Her blue eyes were wide with fear.

''Cos they're daft,' Lizzie said, hooking her arm round Nora. 'There's no such thing as ghosts. He's flesh and blood like anyone else.' She'd never believed in superstitious nonsense and she wasn't about to start now.

CHAPTER 4

'You've settled in, then?'

Mr Fitzgerald's voice made Lizzie jump. She scrambled to her feet. 'They've been heavenly kind, Mr Fitzgerald.'

'Call me Fitzy. Everyone else does.' Mr Fitzgerald lifted his top hat to Mr Sullivan. 'Thanks for feeding an extra mouth, Rory.'

Mr Sullivan shook out his paper. 'One more makes no difference.'

'She's gonna stay with us,' Nora chimed. 'There's room in our bunk.'

'Glad to hear it.' Mr Fitzgerald reached into his

jacket pocket and drew out a roll of papers. 'Now, Lizzie, I want you to go and paste up some bills round town.'

Nora clapped her hands. 'Can we help?'

'I've got flour paste in the bellybox!' Erin dived beneath the wagon and wriggled out a moment later holding a jam jar and a paintbrush. 'Leftovers from sticking last week's clippings in the scrapbook.'

'If there's three of you, sell some tickets while you're out.' Mr Fitzgerald pulled a roll from his pocket and gave them to Lizzie. 'Threepence a ticket…'

'…five for a shilling,' Lizzie chanted.

Mr Fitzgerald winked. 'Exactly.'

Pa Sullivan wagged a finger at Erin and Nora. 'Make sure you're back in time for practice.'

'Yes, Pa!' Erin was already dashing away over the grass, Nora at her heels.

Lizzie raced after them, puffing by the time she reached the park gates where Erin and Nora were already pasting a bill onto a pillar:

Fitzy's Travelling Circus
Every Evening at Dusk
The Astonishing Boissets

Mario the Mighty
Sullivans' Bareback Balleta

'That's us, that is.' Nora pointed to the Balleta. 'We perform a whole ballet on horseback, costume changes an' all.'

'Who's he?' Lizzie pointed to a handsome young man, one of the Astonishing Boissets. With dark hair and shining eyes, he looked like a prince.

Erin and Nora looked at one another and giggled.

'Tell me!' Lizzie said, growing a little hot in the face.

'Tell you? We'll introduce you,' Nora smirked.

'Keep a look out, Lizzie.' Erin slapped another brushful of paste over the poster, covering the handsome youth with a blob of gloop. 'Police don't like us bill-sticking.'

'Leave it to me.' Lizzie was used to playing lookout. She'd kept watch for Pa often enough while he'd been pulling one of his begging scams. She backed out into the road till she had a clear view down both sides of the park and could glance over her shoulder and see right down Oxford Street. There was no sign of a blue uniform among the shoppers on Oxford Street, and the pavements beside the park were empty except for the occasional stroller or a nanny out for a bit of early morning air. 'If I see a rozzer I'll do this.' Lizzie whistled a shrill warning.

Nora grinned. 'I think we'll hear that a mile off.'

Lizzie spotted a smartly dressed gent on Oxford Street. 'Circus ticket, sir?' She crossed the road and fell into step beside him. 'I'm sure your family would love to watch the World-Famous Bareback Balleta.' The gent slowed. Lizzie tore off five tickets. 'There's acrobats and elephants and hump-backed horses.'

'Hump-backed horses?' The gent stopped.

'Like horses, but bigger and *much* humpier,' Lizzie assured him. 'I seen them m'self. Big long noses and goo-goo eyes.' She pulled a face, trying to show him how the odd animals had looked at her last night.

The gent suddenly smiled. 'I think my family would enjoy seeing humpy horses with goo-goo eyes.'

'Five tickets for a shilling.' Lizzie held up the tickets and took his shilling. 'Thank you kindly, sir.' Grinning, she checked the roads again for rozzers and headed toward another shopper. 'Circus tickets, five for a shilling!'

*   *   *

Back at the circus, Lizzie jingled her dress pockets as she followed Fitzy around the outside of the big tent. They were heavy with coins. 'I sold 'em all.'

'I'm impressed!' Fitzy stepped over a guy rope and tugged it to make sure it was taut. 'You're a natural.'

'What can I do now?' Lizzie asked.

'Dump your coins there.' Fitzy spread a handkerchief on the grass. 'Then go give Anita a hand.' He waved toward the Ten-in-One tent.

Lizzie emptied her pockets and hared away, dodging between the stalls until she reached the Ten in One sideshow. As she burst through the door, Anita spun round on her stage. 'Hello,' Lizzie panted. 'Fitzy sent me to help.' She glanced around the empty stages. 'Where is everyone?'

'The show don't open till dusk.' Anita put her hands on her hips. 'Hang about, I've seen you before, haven't I? You was in the audience last night.'

'I'm Lizzie.' She climbed onto the stage beside Anita.

The tiny woman waved toward her backdrop. 'That needs changing. It's filthy but I can't reach the 'ooks.'

Lizzie reached up and began unhooking the backdrop from its hanger, keeping her eyes on her work. Anita was so small that she only reached Lizzie's waist, and Lizzie paused and snatched a look at her. 'I hope you don't mind my asking, but how come you're so tiny?'

'Never grew much since I was born.' Anita sat down in her chair and pointed up at the backdrop. 'Carry on with your unpinnin'.'

Lizzie quickly turned back to her work. 'Don't you hate it, sitting here, being stared at by strangers?' She shuddered. '*I'd* hate it.'

'I did, to begin with,' Anita admitted. 'But I'm used to it now. There's folks here who look out for me. Life here ain't as tough as it was out there.'

Lizzie glanced over her shoulder. 'What did you do?' she asked. 'Out there?' She wondered if Anita had lived anywhere as stinking as Rat's Castle.

'I did what I could,' Anita told her. 'Beggin', mainly. No one'd give me proper work. And beggin' was no picnic. People used to throw things at me, kick me if they could. Once someone even picked me up and threw me. Like I was no more than a dog.'

'Why do people have to be mean?' Lizzie unhooked the last hook and laid the backdrop on the stage.

Anita pointed to a fresh backdrop folded beside her chair. 'I guess they don't know no better.'

Lizzie scooped it up and began hooking as Anita went on.

'I'm glad Fitzy found me,' the tiny woman told her. 'Saw me beggin' and asked me to join 'is circus. Of course, I'd rather be a lady livin' in a big house with servants and all that, but I'm safe in my penny gaff.'

Lizzie paused. 'What's a penny gaff?'

'You're standing in one,' Anita told her. 'It's a sideshow. Something a person would pay a penny to see.' A loud bell clanged outside and Anita hopped off her chair. 'That's Fitzy. Sounds like he's got an announcement.'

Lizzie quickly finished hooking up the backdrop, then jumped down after Anita and crossed the field to where Fitzy was standing outside the big show tent.

The Fat Lady stood puffing beside him while the Amazon Queen sat on a barrel sewing fresh feathers into her headdress. Show folk streamed from every wagon and tent, and Lizzie recognized the acrobats and clowns from the parade. Dwarves toddled beside giants. A boy on stilts stopped and leaned against a guy rope.

'Lizzie!' Erin and Nora came running across the grass.

Lizzie rushed to meet them. 'What's Fitzy want?'

'Dunno.' Erin shrugged.

'The mayor's here.' Malachy ducked under a guy rope and stopped beside them. 'He's come to see Pop.'

'The Mayor of London?' Lizzie gasped. 'Here?'

Erin and Nora grinned. 'Pa said he'd come.'

'He's made friends with Pop,' Malachy explained.

'Where is he?' Lizzie scanned the crowd until she saw an old gentleman step from the shadows behind Fitzy. Erin gave a loud whistle and Malachy hooted as the crowd erupted into cheers:

'Hurray for His Lordship!'

'Long live the mayor!'

Lizzie stared open-mouthed – it was the old gentleman who'd given her soup and the penny. *The Lord Mayor of London!*

The mayor waved the crowd into silence. 'Thank you for your warm welcome. I've come to tell you that when you set up at Victoria Park next month, I will lead the official opening ceremony!'

As the show folk burst into more cheering, Fitzy stepped forward and shouted over them, 'Three cheers for the mayor!'

'Hip hip hooray!' Lizzie shouted with the crowd.

'Hip hip hooray!'

'Hip hip hooray!'

'The mayor's support will mean bigger audiences,' Fitzy went on. 'And better write-ups in the press – Victoria Park will be our best show ever!'

Malachy whispered in Lizzie's ear, 'The papers don't usually have anything good to say about us circus folk.'

'Now, back to work.' Fitzy looked at his pocketwatch. 'The first show starts in four hours.'

As the crowd melted away, Malachy glanced at Lizzie. 'How are you enjoying circus life?'

'It's brilliant!' Lizzie winked. 'Almost worth being poked awake with a stick.' Malachy looked sheepish and Lizzie gave him a nudge. 'I'm just joshing,' she told him. 'I never thanked you properly for persuading your pa to take me on.'

Malachy shrugged. 'You're welcome.' Lizzie thought she saw him blush as he turned and hobbled away between the booths.

Erin tugged Lizzie's sleeves. 'You're coming to watch us practise, aren't you?'

'Next time,' Lizzie promised. Right now, she wanted to make herself as useful as she could. She began to pick her way round the show tent, hopping over the guy ropes until she spotted a tall man heaving a tall pole onto its end. She rushed to help. 'Let me hold it.' She ducked under the man's elbow and clung onto the pole, holding it in place while the man fixed its guy ropes onto pegs.

'You're strong for a little 'un.' The man's voice was deep. Lizzie glanced at him and suddenly realized he was the tallest man she'd ever seen. He held out a huge hand for her to shake. 'I'm Mario.'

Lizzie stared up at him. 'Mario the Mighty! From the poster! You're the circus giant.'

He must be ten feet tall! She wondered what he'd look like standing next to Anita.

He nodded toward another tent pole. 'If I lift that into place can you do some more holding while I fix the ropes?'

Lizzie nodded and braced herself, ready to take the weight of the pole as Mario heaved it up onto its end.

'Did you hear about the mayor?' Mario asked as he looped a guy rope around a peg.

Lizzie nodded and hugged the pole. 'It's great that he's opening the circus in Victoria Park.'

'If that don't bring the crowds in, nothing will.' Mario grinned. 'The mayor's a good 'un. He knows what it's like to come from poverty.'

Lizzie pricked her ears. 'Really?' She remembered the rookery twang in his voice.

'He was raised in Jacob's Island.'

Jacob's Island. It was more of a slum than Rat's Castle. Pa used to say, 'Just be grateful you ain't stuck in Jacob's Island. They feeds their babies to dogs there.'

She shivered. 'How did he get out?'

'He worked his way out,' Mario told her. 'From errand boy to mayor, and not a false step in between.'

'I seen him the first night I was here,' Lizzie told Mario. 'He gave me soup and a penny. Best soup I ever tasted. I was starving.'

Mario looked at her quizzically. 'Where are you from?'

'Rat's Castle.'

'You're better off here.' Mario lifted another tent pole.

Lizzie rushed to help balance it. 'Don't I know it!'

'Poverty can do evil things to a man's soul.'

Lizzie thought of Pa and shuddered.

* * *

'Is Harry here?' Lizzie peeked through the tent doorway. A foul stink hit her nose and she covered it with her hand.

A boy was sitting on a stool beside an elephant. 'I'm Hari.'

'Hari.' Lizzie repeated the name, copying the boy's soft accent. It felt clumsy on her tongue.

'It's Indian,' Hari explained.

'Oh.' Lizzie stepped inside. She knew India was part of the Empire but she'd never met an Indian before. She bowed awkwardly. 'Do you speak English?'

Hari smiled. 'Yes. Do you?'

Lizzie flushed. 'Of course.' The elephant behind Hari shifted on the straw and she backed away. 'He's not gonna tread on me, is he?'

Hari laughed. 'No. And, by the way, he's a *she*.'

'I ain't stayin' if you're gonna laugh!' Lizzie said. 'How was I meant to know? They don't have bloomin' great elephants where I come from!'

It was the end of a long day. Dusk was falling and the crowds were gathering outside. Fitzy had told her to come and help Hari so she'd come.

Hari stroked the elephant's trunk gently. 'I'm sorry.' His brown eyes softened. 'I know elephants make people nervous.'

'They're just so big,' Lizzie said, lifting her chin.

'This is Akula.' Hari beckoned Lizzie closer. 'Come and give her a stroke.'

Lizzie had seen the elephant before, going for her bath. She was huge. As Lizzie eyed the enormous animal warily, another shape moved in the shadows on the other side of the tent and Lizzie stiffened as she realized it was a second elephant.

'That's Sashi,' Hari told her. 'They're very gentle,' he promised. 'Come.' He beckoned again. 'Come stroke Akula on her trunk – that's her nose.'

Reluctantly, Lizzie stepped forward and reached out a hand. She was determined not to tremble, but her fingers quivered as they neared Akula's trunk.

'She likes to be stroked,' Hari reassured her.

Gently, Lizzie touched Akula's trunk. It felt dry and warm. Akula stood still while Lizzie ran her fingers over the rough hide.

'See?' Hari reached up and scratched Akula behind her ear.

Akula curled the end of her trunk and Lizzie saw its soft pink tip. *Imagine having a nose that long*, she thought.

Hari grinned as Akula lifted it higher and began to sniff Lizzie.

Lizzie forced herself not to run as the elephant ran the snuffling tip of her trunk over her. 'Hello, Akula.' She stroked her trunk. 'I'm new here. I guess I smell funny.'

Akula lifted her trunk higher and puffed air into Lizzie's face. Lizzie hopped backward in surprise.

'She likes you!' Hari laughed.

'Really?' Lizzie looked at him.

'Really.' Hari picked up a short, stout stool and put it beside Akula's foreleg. 'Come on, girl.'

'What are you doing?'

'We have to file their toenails before the show,' Hari explained.

'File their toenails?' Lizzie echoed. 'What with?'

Hari lifted a large iron file from the straw. 'This.' He tapped the back of Akula's leg. 'Come on, girl.'

Akula lifted her foreleg and placed it on the stool. Bending down, Hari began to file her huge toenails.

Lizzie watched, amazed, as the file sent a shower of dust onto the straw. Hari worked steadily and quietly. There was a calmness about him that put Lizzie at her ease. 'How did you know the elephants made me nervous?' she asked.

'People often get cross when they're scared.' Hari kept gently filing one nail after another. 'Next leg, girl.' He tapped Akula and she swapped legs.

Lizzie crouched down in the straw and cupped her chin in her hands. Hari was a slender boy with smooth brown skin and the darkest eyes Lizzie had ever seen. His black hair curled softly at his neck as he worked.

'Do you want to try?' he asked suddenly.

Lizzie blinked. 'I d-don't know.'

Hari held the file out. Lizzie took it and approached Akula's huge foot. Tentatively, she gave one of the toenails a swish with the file. It slid over the nail.

'Harder,' Hari encouraged.

Lizzie swished the file again, more firmly. This time dust showered from the nail. Akula swayed beside Lizzie but didn't move her foot.

'That's perfect,' Hari murmured.

Lizzie began filing the nail where it hung over the edge of Akula's pad. She was concentrating so hard she barely felt Akula's trunk snuffling her back.

'There,' she said at last, straightening and admiring her work. Akula's toenails were short and smooth. She gave the file back to Hari. 'You'd better do the back ones,' she said. 'I don't know how to make her swap legs.' She sat in the straw while Hari moved the stool and began filing the toenails on Akula's hind legs, and suddenly realized how quiet it was here. Outside, the circus was bustling, but Hari was alone in the elephant tent. 'Don't you get lonely with just the elephants for company?' she asked.

'I prefer it.' He patted Akula's flank. 'Animals are easier to be around. They never hide what they're really feeling. You never have to guess.'

'I s'pose.' It had always been clear what Pa was feeling – Lizzie touched the bruise on her cheek.

She wondered suddenly about the Phantom. The show folk had been talking about him all day, shocked by the violent turn his crimes had suddenly taken. 'What do you suppose the Phantom is feeling when he commits his crimes?'

Hari went on filing. 'I think he's ashamed.'

'Why?'

'Because he wears a mask. People do that when they're ashamed of themselves.'

Lizzie remembered the ghoulish sketch in the newspaper. 'Do you think it really is a mask?'

'It must be,' Hari insisted. 'That's no human face.'

'Some people are saying he's *not* human.'

'Oh, he's human all right,' Hari argued. '*Very* human. That mask doesn't just cover his shame. It makes him feel bigger and better than he really is. Haven't you noticed how people often use clothes to make themselves look important?'

Lizzie pictured the toffs on Oxford Street, done up in silks and top hats, like they were more important than the beggars and tradesmen who had to wear what was needed rather than what they wanted.

'I hope they catch him soon,' Hari said softly.

'So do I,' Lizzie agreed.

'If he's turned violent, it means that robbery isn't a big enough thrill any more. And if it's excitement he's after, he'll get more and more dangerous.'

Lizzie tucked her knees under her chin and hugged them close. 'I hope not.'

Hari stepped away from Akula and slid the file into his back pocket. He smiled suddenly, his white teeth bright in the dusky light. 'Come on.' He held out his hands, and Lizzie grabbed them and let him pull her up. 'How would you like to sit on an elephant's back?'

Lizzie swallowed. 'I don't know.'

'Here.' Hari tapped Akula's leg and she lifted it. 'Put your foot up here.'

Surprised at herself, Lizzie climbed up onto Akula's knee.

'Up, Akula, up!' As Hari spoke, Akula wrapped her trunk round Lizzie's waist and hoisted her up into the air.

Lizzie gasped as Akula sat her gently down on her back. She stared down at Hari. He seemed a hundred feet away. 'It's so high!' She wanted to laugh with exhilaration. She was sitting on top of an elephant!

'Lizzie?' Erin popped her head round the door.

'What are you doing up there?' Nora had followed her sister into the tent.

'I'm being the Queen of Sheba,' Lizzie told them proudly.

'Come down!' Nora flapped her hands. 'Malachy's bringing someone to meet you!'

'Who?' Lizzie turned onto her belly and let herself slide down Akula's side. She felt Erin and Nora's hands catch her and lower her gently onto the straw.

Malachy's voice sounded from the doorway. 'I would like to present…'

Erin made a drum roll sound while Nora tooted like a trumpet through her hands.

'…the *Great* Dru Boisset!' Malachy waved his arm

with a flourish and the boy from the poster came somersaulting through the doorway. Landing as nimble as a cat, the boy threw out his arms and bowed.

Lizzie stared at him. She'd thought the artist might have exaggerated how good-looking he was, but no – he really was that handsome, his green eyes sparkling in the half-light.

'Are you one of the acrobats?' she asked. It was all she could think of to say.

'An acrobat?' The Great Dru Boisset lifted his hands in mock horror. '*Mais non!*'

Nora and Erin collapsed into giggles, and Malachy gave Dru a playful shove. 'Stop showing off.' He turned to Lizzie. 'Dru works in the high wire act.'

'The high wire!' Lizzie felt dizzy just thinking about it. 'With that lady on the penny farthing?'

'She's my sister, Collette.' Dru flung himself down onto a heap of straw. Erin and Nora curled up next to him, pulling Lizzie down beside them.

'Don't you get scared up there?' Lizzie asked.

Dru shook his head. In perfect English, with the slightest hint of a French accent, he said, 'Up there is the only place I feel like *me*.'

Lizzie glanced at Hari. 'Like Hari with his elephants.'

'And us on horseback!' Nora added.

Malachy sat down. 'I feel happiest with my feet firmly on the ground.' He tapped his club foot with his stick. 'Even if one of them's firmer than the other.'

'Join us, Hari!' Erin called. 'I know we're not elephants but we're nearly as nice.'

Hari grinned and gave Akula a pat, then sat cross-legged beside Nora.

'Right.' Erin leaned forward and stared at Lizzie, eyes bright. 'We want to know all about you.'

'Me?' Lizzie felt suddenly self-conscious.

'Of course!' Nora insisted. 'You're the most exciting thing to happen here for ages!'

'I'm not exciting,' Lizzie told them quickly.

'Of course you are,' Dru argued. 'You are a mystery, appearing from nowhere in the night.'

'Where are you from, Lizzie?' Erin leaned closer.

'A place called Rat's Castle.'

'Rat's Castle?' Nora wrinkled her nose. 'That sounds horrible.' She slapped her hands over her mouth. 'Sorry, I didn't mean to sound rude!'

Lizzie shook her head. 'You're right. It *is* horrible. It's stinky and mean and full of beggars and thieves and there's no one magic like you lot.'

Malachy tipped his head to one side. 'Is that why you ran away?'

Before Lizzie could answer, Hari's steady gaze fixed on her. 'What about your family, Lizzie? Won't they miss you?'

Lizzie looked down. 'My mother and brother are dead.'

Hari's eyes grew round with sympathy. 'My mother is dead too.'

'So's mine,' Malachy sighed.

Lizzie touched the bruise on her cheek. 'And Pa...' she hesitated. 'Pa's just... Pa.'

'Oh, Lizzie!' Nora flung her arms round her. 'You poor thing!'

'I'm not a poor thing! Look!' Lizzie shook her off. 'Look where I am! I'm not poor at all.'

Later, as the crowds faded and the circus grew quiet, Lizzie snuggled deep into her bunk beside Nora and Erin. The Sullivans snored and mumbled around her, tucked above and below like loaves in an oven. For the first time since Ma died, Lizzie felt safe and warm.

Smiling to herself, she closed her eyes. She was soon dreaming of high wires and elephants.

Swooping from a trapeze she landed lightly on her feet in the elephant tent. Akula lifted her trunk to greet her but, as Lizzie reached out her hand to stroke the gentle creature, she vanished into darkness.

Lizzie spun round. Shadows swamped every corner.

'Akula?' Lizzie strained to see. 'Hari?'

'Lizzie,' a voice answered back.

'Who's there?' Lizzie tiptoed forward.

'Are you looking for me?'

Lizzie's heart quickened as she heard rasping breathing ahead.

A face loomed from the shadows.

The Phantom!

Snarling, he lunged. His black cloak fluttered as he flew at her. He slammed into her and she staggered backward...

As she hit the ground, Lizzie woke with a gasp.

Nora moved beside her and sighed. Around her the Sullivans still snored and mumbled in their sleep. Relieved, Lizzie let herself sink into the soft mattress, her heart slowing as she drifted back into sleep.

CHAPTER 5

The next morning, the hustle and bustle of the Sullivan family's caravan made it easy for Lizzie to forget her nightmare about the Phantom.

'Come on!' Erin tugged Lizzie out of the caravan while Nora raced behind.

'Why won't you just tell me what they're called?' Lizzie leaped a guy rope as Erin swung her past the Lobster Boy's penny gaff.

'I will, when we get there!' Erin dodged past the elephant tent.

Lizzie had been asking about the humpback horses over breakfast in the caravan. 'Humpback horses!' Nora and Erin had burst into fits of giggles.

Patrick, shovelling in porridge at the far end of the table, had choked with laughter while Ma and Pa Sullivan exchanged smiles across Pa's newspaper.

'We'll get to the humpbacks in just a while.' Erin skidded to a halt beside the horse pen.

Conor was brushing down his golden mare at the far side. 'Don't be expecting me to brush Marigold and Daisy down for you again today.' He waved his brush at them. 'I've got to practise my somersaults. I've no time for grooming.'

'I hear you,' Erin hollered back. 'We're just showing Lizzie the animals.' She was ready with a sugar lump as her pony came trotting to meet her. 'There you go, Marigold.' She stood on the bottom rung of the fence and leaned over. Marigold whickered and nibbled it softly from her palm.

'Hello, Daisy.' Nora climbed the rail beside them and took a sugar lump from her pocket as her pony nudged Marigold aside. 'Here, Lizzie. You give it her. Rest it on your palm and keep your thumb tucked in,' she advised.

Lizzie held her hand out gingerly, thumb tucked in. She felt the pony's warm breath as it nuzzled her palm and softly took the sugar.

'Good girl, Daisy.' Nora patted the pony's neck.

Lizzie gazed across the pen. 'Where are the humpbacks?'

'They're called camels.' A deep voice sounded from the pen beside them. Mario, the circus giant, was leaning over the fence. 'Come round and say hello. I'm just about to feed them.'

Lizzie clambered over the fence and jumped down beside Mario. 'That's them!' She pointed excitedly at the two camels grazing on the far side of the pen. They looked even stranger in the sunshine, their brown pelts shaggy and their humps tufted and floppy at the top.

'Wait here.' Mario held up a hand as Erin and Nora leaped down beside Lizzie. 'Camels can be grumpy first thing in the morning and when they're grumpy, they spit.'

'Like Pa,' Lizzie muttered.

Erin nudged her. 'Conor's a champion spitter, so he is.'

'He can spit the length of the circus ring,' Nora boasted.

'Can you spit, Lizzie?' Erin looked at her with round eyes.

Lizzie grinned. 'I could knock a fly outta the air if I

wanted.' She left Nora and Erin exchanging impressed glances as she hurried after Mario. He was beckoning from beside the camels as they leaned down and munched hay from the pile he'd scattered at their feet. 'This is Sultan.' He scratched the thick pelt of one of the camels. 'And this is his partner Sabira.'

Sabira lifted her head and blinked.

'Look at her eyelashes! They're so long.' Lizzie pointed at the drooping hump. 'And what's that for?'

'To store water in.' Mario patted Sultan. 'For long treks across the desert.' He winked. 'D'you want to see something better?'

'Better than camels?' Lizzie followed Mario out of the pen and past the show tent. Beyond the guy ropes, she could see the King of the Jungle's cage where a golden pelt stretched on a carpet of straw. 'Is that Leo?' She raced to the pen and peered through the bars.

The lion lifted his wide head and shook out his mane.

'You've heard about him, then?' Mario crouched down beside her and stuck his fingers through the bars.

'So it's true he's old and got no teeth!' Lizzie said. The big cat was so handsome. 'Poor ol' thing.'

'He's had a good life,' Mario assured her. 'Been

with Fitzy since he was a cub. Lost his teeth from too much candyfloss.'

Leo leaned forward and licked Mario's fingers with a massive tongue.

'He's a pussycat!' Lizzie giggled.

Erin and Nora caught them up. 'Are you still scared of Leo?' Nora teased. Leo stretched out and flexed his claws. They were like butcher's hooks.

'I wouldn't get in a cage with him.' Lizzie gazed at Leo. 'Who does?'

'Fitzy,' Erin crouched beside her. 'He's Fitzy's act. He has Leo jumping through hoops every show. The crowd love it. Leo acts all fierce and then Fitzy acts fiercer.'

'It's just a big game for them both,' Nora said with a grin. 'They're old friends.'

'Come on.' Erin jumped to her feet. 'Let's leave Leo in peace and watch Dru practise.'

'Lawks, yes!' Lizzie hadn't seen the high wire act yet. She chased after Erin, tugging Nora by the hand. 'Thanks, Mario!' she called over her shoulder.

They ducked into the show tent, where the smell of sawdust and canvas filled Lizzie's nose. She hadn't seen the show yet – she'd been too busy helping the performers – but she'd peeked inside the red and black striped tent on her way to fetch pegs for Mario yesterday. This was the first time she'd been right inside, though.

Malachy was sitting on the brightly painted step that ringed the wide stretch of sawdust. Clowns cavorted and tumbled in the middle. Lizzie laughed as one pulled the hat of another down over his face. Water shot out of the top.

'Look!' Erin pointed at the roof.

Lizzie craned her neck and saw Dru waving from a platform high up on a fat tent pole. Arms stretched out, he stepped out onto a wire strung across the ring and walked across.

Lizzie swallowed. 'What if he falls?'

'He'll die.' A voice sounded behind her and Lizzie swung round. The girl in spangled tights she'd seen yesterday with the penny farthing bicycle was standing behind them. It was Dru's sister, Collette.

Lizzie searched Collette's face. It was gaudy with makeup and pretty as a doll's. But no worry showed in her round blue eyes. *Doesn't she love her brother?* thought Lizzie.

Malachy leaned forward on his cane. 'No one's ever died at Fitzy's circus,' he told Lizzie. 'And Fitzy says

Dru can have a safety net if he wants.'

'I wish he would.' Nora clasped her hands together.

Erin sighed. 'He says safety nets are for kids.'

'But he's hardly more than a kid, ain't he?' Lizzie looked up, relieved, as Dru reached the far platform.

Collette shrugged. 'He's old enough to earn his own living.'

Dru was shinning down the tent pole. He leaped the last few feet and raced across the ring. 'Impressed?' He stopped beside Lizzie.

Lizzie was about to answer when a figure caught her eye. Marching into the ring was a woman. At least, she was *dressed* like a woman. But a handsome beard covered her cheeks and hair sprouted from her neck and arms as thickly as if she was wearing fur. She stopped beside a short fat clown, grabbed him by the lapels and kissed him hard.

'That's Ursula!' Erin followed her gaze. 'The Bear Woman.'

Lizzie stared. 'Why's she kissing clowns?'

'That's her husband, Rice Pudding Pete,' Nora told her.

'Rice Pudding Pete?' Lizzie echoed.

Erin sat down beside Malachy. 'He closes the act by

falling into a vat of rice pudding.'

Dru ducked in front of Lizzie, blocking her view. 'My act? What did you think?'

Lizzie blinked into Dru's green eyes. 'It was amazing! I could hardly breathe. How d'you keep your balance?'

Dru ran his fingers through his hair. 'Practice.'

Collette frowned at Ursula. 'She should be in her booth with the other freaks, not in here with the *performers*.'

Lizzie felt a surge of annoyance. *How dare she?* Anita's words rang in her mind: *People used to throw things at me, kick me if they could. Like I was no more than a dog.* Before she could stop herself, she burst out with, 'Who are you calling a freak?' She looked Collette up and down. 'Standing there in your underwear! They're people, just like you an' me!'

Just then Lizzie saw Fitzy standing behind Collette. Oh no! Was he going to be furious with her for shouting at one of the stars? She shut up quickly.

But Fitzy was smiling. 'Well said, Lizzie. We're a family here at Fitzy's circus.' He flashed a stern look at Collette. 'We may bicker, but no one is more important than anyone else and we look after each other, right?'

Collette looked at him from under her lashes.

'Right,' she muttered sulkily.

'Go and get on with your practice.' He shooed her away and fixed his gaze on Lizzie. 'I've got a special job for you.'

Lizzie straightened. Did someone need her to fix their stage or iron their costume? 'I'm ready.'

Fitzy smiled. 'Good.' He glanced down at her dress – the same shabby grey frock she'd been wearing since she'd arrived. 'Erin!' he called over his shoulder. 'You're about the same size as Lizzie. Can she borrow your Sunday dress?'

'Of course.' Erin nodded. 'Why? Is she going to church?'

'Not quite.' Fitzy started to lead Lizzie out of the tent. 'Madame Aurora needs an assistant.'

As visitors started streaming toward the circus, Lizzie stood beside the Sullivans' caravan in Erin's Sunday best, chestnut brown hair stiffly plaited, feeling as trussed up as a Christmas goose.

'Mercy, Lizzie,' Nora giggled. She handed her Ma Sullivan's ivory-back mirror. The black taffeta made

Lizzie look white as a ghost and her face was pale above the stiff collar.

Lizzie scowled. 'I look like I'm off to a funeral.'

'You might as well be,' Erin told her gravely.

Nora grasped her hand. 'Be good,' she warned. 'Madame Aurora can be an awful banshee.'

'She's a bit cantankerous,' Fitzy explained as he led Lizzie toward Madame Aurora's tent. 'But do as you're told and you'll be right as rain. Just stand there and look mournful while Madame A's doing her readings.' He stopped outside a tent and lifted the flap. 'She does palms and cards and the old crystal ball. You know the kind of thing. She just needs you looking maudlin to help add a little solemnity to proceedings.' He called inside. 'Madame Aurora, your new assistant is here.'

Lizzie peered into the shadows. Exotic perfume filled her nose. An oil lamp, turned low, barely lit the luxurious drapes that swathed the inside of the tent.

'Send her in.' A sultry voice sounded in the dim light.

As Lizzie stepped inside, she could make out a figure seated at a table, then Madame Aurora rose regally, shimmering with sequins and jingling with jewellery. A blood-red veil covered her face. She lifted it and Lizzie saw the strong features of a handsome woman, caked with make-up.

'Not much of a girl.' Madame Aurora poked Lizzie's shoulder with a bony finger. The nail dug deep beneath Lizzie's shoulder bone.

Lizzie flinched but held her tongue. She wasn't going to risk losing her first proper job in the circus.

Madame Aurora lifted one of Lizzie's plaits and let it fall from her fingers like a dead mouse. 'Couldn't you find anyone more exotic?' she asked stonily. 'This one looks like she's fresh from the workhouse.'

Fitzy put his hand gently on Lizzie's shoulder. 'She's a good worker and she's bright. Her looks will improve once we've fed her up a bit.'

Lizzie dug her nails deep into her palms. *Why do grown-ups have to be so rude? Like kids don't have proper feelings.*

Madame Aurora tossed her headscarf back and turned to her table. 'I'll do what I can with her.' She pointed to the doorway. 'Stand there, girl.'

'My name's Lizzie.' Lizzie lifted her chin.

'While you're working here, you're called Roxanna.' Madame Aurora sat down and gazed into the crystal ball sitting on her table, her ringed fingers fluttering around it. 'Guide the client in, show them to their seat, then stand back and keep your mouth shut. I don't want them knowing you're a guttersnipe from the slums.'

Lizzie flashed Fitzy a worried look as he hovered outside the doorway.

'You'll do fine.' He glanced over his shoulder. 'Here comes your first pheasant for plucking.'

Madame Aurora quickly pulled her veil down over her face as Fitzy hurried away. A young woman was approaching the tent warily. Her eyes were red, her nose rosy from crying. Lizzie beckoned her in and the young woman offered her a coin, but Madame Aurora's voice called out, smooth as honey, 'I'll take your coin, dear. The spirits won't speak unless you cross my palm with silver.'

Lizzie ushered the woman to the empty chair opposite Madame Aurora and, as the woman sat down, stepped back into the shadows. She watched as Madame Aurora pocketed the coin.

'Why have you come to seek guidance from the spirit world?' Madame Aurora's veil trembled.

You should know, Lizzie thought. *You're meant to be psychic.* She shuffled her feet.

Madame jerked her head in Lizzie's direction. 'Stand

still!' she hissed.

As Madame turned back toward her client, Lizzie stuck out her tongue. Madame Aurora didn't see, her gaze being fixed on the young woman who was dabbing her nose with a handkerchief. 'You seem troubled, my dear.'

The woman nodded.

Well, that's obvious!

Madame stroked the air around her crystal ball. 'I see heartache.'

The woman sniffed and wrung her hanky between her fingers.

'Let me see.' Madame Aurora gently lifted one of the woman's hands and turned her palm upward. Leaning over it she mumbled and shook her head. 'You have known sorrow.'

The woman sniffed again.

'Your love line is broken, see?' Madame Aurora pointed toward the woman's palm.

The woman looked closer. 'I've been let down,' she confessed.

'A man you trusted has abandoned you.'

As Madame Aurora spoke, the woman swallowed back a sob. 'Archibald.'

'He was not the man for you,' Madame Aurora assured her. 'Look.' She ran a finger over the woman's palm. 'Beyond the break, the line runs long and smooth. Another man waits, more trustworthy and with a faithful heart. You will find your true happiness with him.'

Can she really tell that just by looking at her palm? Lizzie wondered, but she saw the young woman's shoulders rise as though a great weight had been lifted from them.

'Thank you!' The young woman stood up and began to back out. 'Thank you so much.'

Lizzie quickly stepped forward to pull the curtain aside. Another client was waiting outside – a man this time, his forehead furrowed. He hardly acknowledged Lizzie as she waved him toward the chair.

Madame Aurora looked him over and Lizzie followed her gaze as it lingered on his frayed collar and the threadbare hat he rolled in his hands.

She gazed into her crystal ball. 'Financial worries weigh heavily on you.' The man nodded.

Even I could tell that by just looking!

'But fortune awaits.' Madame Aurora peered harder into her ball.

'Fortune?' The man sat forward in his chair and Madame held out her palm.

The man reached into his pocket and handed her a coin at once. 'What fortune?'

'Fortune beyond your wildest imaginings,' Madame Aurora promised. 'In business, your path is assured. I see water.' She lifted her veil and peered even closer into the crystal. 'Great oceans bearing great ships.'

'Should I invest in shipping?' In the dim light, Lizzie could see the back of the man's neck flush with excitement.

'Your fortune will come from overseas,' Madame Aurora's voice deepened.

She's just telling him what he wants to hear! Lizzie wanted to warn the man not to trust Madame Aurora's advice. But if she did, she'd lose her job; maybe even her place in the circus. She bit her lip and stayed quiet as Madame Aurora went on.

'Great wealth is within your reach, you need only wait and it will fall into your lap.'

The man was fidgeting with excitement. 'Thank you, Missus Aurora.' He grabbed her hand and shook it, then jumped to his feet. He was out of the tent before Lizzie had time to lift the door.

'How can you get him all worked up like that?' Lizzie demanded.

Madame Aurora lifted her head. 'I only tell what the spirits instruct,' she murmured.

'Sure you do,' Lizzie muttered as she lifted the flap for the next client.

'She makes it all up, I swear!' Lizzie paced back and forth beside Akula while Erin, Nora, Malachy and Hari lounged in the hay. The last show had finished; chores were done. Before long, Ma Sullivan would be shouting them back to the caravan for bed. Lizzie grabbed an old straw sack from the floor and draped it like a veil over her head. 'You are troubled, dear...' Copying Madame Aurora's throaty whisper, she knelt beside Malachy and peered into his palm. 'I see from your life line that you are young. But don't worry ... you'll get older!' She grabbed Erin's hand. 'You are troubled, dear. You have to sleep in a caravan with four snoring brothers.' She grasped Hari's hand. 'I see in your love line that your next sweetheart will be an heiress and you will live in the best houses and eat only the best food.'

As her friends hooted with laughter, Lizzie straightened. 'But the best was the toffs. She took longest with the toffs. I expect she thought she was going to get an extra shilling. Mercy, did she ask them questions! As soon as a smart suit comes through the door, she's telling them they'll win big on the stock market and then asking them where their houses are and where they work. Do you know what she said?' Lizzie put on the haughty voice of Madame Aurora again: '"Once I am certain of your geographical location, the spirits speak to me stronger." And then the toffs'd say where they lived and talk about their job in some bank or other and she'd um and ah and say, "Of course. I feel it now. An inheritance is coming your way," or "Your wife will give you a son before the year is out to carry on your noble line."' Lizzie flopped down into the straw beside Erin. 'I thought she was gonna do real magic. But it's all make-believe.' She sighed.

Erin rubbed her back. 'That's the circus, Lizzie. It's all a big illusion.'

'But *Anita's* real,' Lizzie pointed out.

Malachy shifted beside Hari. 'She's about the only one who is. The Pig-Faced Woman's an old bear in a dress with a shaved face.'

Lizzie gaped at him. 'What about the mermaid?'

'Fake tail made out of walrus hide,' Nora laughed. 'And Sid the Lobster Boy's never even seen the sea. He was just born with his fingers and toes fused together.'

Lizzie heart sank. 'So they're just scamming, like Pa?'

'They're just making the best of what God gave them,' Nora told her. 'People like to see a show, so we give them a show.'

Erin nodded. 'A good show is a sure way to take folks' minds off their troubles.'

'Madame Aurora certainly did that.' Lizzie lay back in the straw. 'Not one punter got bad news. They all left thinking they was gonna fall in love or find a fortune.'

Hari lowered his dark lashes. 'Isn't that better?' he said softly. 'To believe that something wonderful's going to happen. Isn't that better than always worrying about the future?'

'I guess.' Lizzie shrugged. 'And I s'pose, sometimes, she may be right. Though if she'd told me a week ago I'd be working in a circus, I'd never have believed her in a million years.'

'If you can call it working,' said Collette. She had slipped in silently. Lizzie clenched her fists but kept her mouth shut. Collette gave a dazzling smile and clapped her hands. 'You're summoned, boys and girls. Hurry up! To the main tent!'

'What for?' Lizzie was instantly suspicious.

'So my brother can show off his new trick, of course.' Collette's smile never faltered. 'You aren't going to keep him waiting, are you?'

The others leaped to their feet and scrambled out. Lizzie followed, not really wanting to go, but not quite knowing why. Dru was agile and clever, wasn't he? He couldn't be in any danger…

So why was a tight knot of fear growing in her stomach?

'You mustn't mind Collette,' Hari said as she caught up.

'I don't,' Lizzie snapped.

Inside the huge tent it was gloomy and full of shadows. By day it had been a jolly place, but now that the audience had all gone home it seemed sad. Lizzie's creepy feeling grew worse.

Dru was standing at one end of the high wire, grinning down at her. In his pale costume, he looked like a ghost up there in the dark.

'And now, for your delight and delectation,' he called out, 'I shall demonstrate a brand-new feat, never before seen in this circus!'

Erin gasped and nudged her sister excitedly. Malachy watched, wide-eyed. They all seemed transfixed as Dru stepped out onto the wire, arms outstretched. One careful footstep followed another. The wire wobbled beneath him.

'Come down!' The words burst out of Lizzie's mouth before she could stop them. 'It ain't safe!'

'Have no fear,' Dru said, as if he were talking to an audience and not to Lizzie. 'I've practised this one for hours on the training wire.'

He was nearly at the middle of the wire now. It bowed under his weight.

Lizzie's heart pounded like a big bass drum. She had to make Dru stop, somehow. 'You tell him!' she told Collette, rounding on the startled girl. 'Tell him not to do it!'

'My brother is a professional. You're insulting his talent,' Collette said softly.

Now Lizzie's palms were aching. The feeling of horror was taking over her whole body. 'Come down!' she yelled again. Dru's life depended on it. She didn't know how she knew. She just *knew*.

'You'd better hush up, Lizzie,' Malachy whispered.

'You might put him off with that yelling.'

'Something bad's going to happen,' she muttered. 'I just *know* it.'

High above, Dru bent his knees. 'A roll on the drums, please!'

Erin and Nora began to hammer with their hands on the hollow wooden step, and Lizzie could only look on helplessly as Dru bent his knees again and flipped up into the air. The high wire twanged beneath his body as he turned a full backward somersault. Lizzie bit her knuckle.

Dru's feet came down on the wire. It wobbled madly. He swayed his body from side to side, struggling to keep his balance.

Next moment, with a sickening snap, the wire broke loose at one end. Its whole length rippled as it fell, taking Dru with it.

He tumbled, arms flailing, down towards his death.

CHAPTER 6

With an acrobat's reflexes, Dru grabbed for the wire. He caught it and held tight as it swung down, bringing him with it like a huge pendulum.

Everyone rushed forwards. They gathered below the tent pole as Dru, white-faced, inched his way down the wire. He dropped the last few feet and stood there trembling with shock.

'I'm all right,' he said, waving away their anxious questions. 'These things happen.'

'Not in this circus they don't!' Collette burst out. 'This was no accident. Someone sabotaged that wire!' She turned on Lizzie. 'It was you, wasn't it? You meant that to happen to *me*!'

'I never!' Lizzie yelled.

'Oh no? Then how did you know my brother was in danger, eh?'

'I…' The words stuck in her throat. How could she possibly explain? 'I just had a feeling.'

Collette just snorted at that.

Lizzie turned around, desperate for backup, but Nora and Erin were looking at her with doubtful faces. Surely they couldn't think she was responsible…

But it was Hari who came to her rescue. 'I think you should all look at this,' he said quietly. He held up the end of the fallen high wire, which was frayed and discoloured.

'Mildew,' said Dru, shaking his head. 'It must have been rotting through for weeks. Collette, how many times have I said we need a new rope?'

Lizzie folded her arms. 'I'm waiting for an apology.'

Collette stared at Lizzie as if she were suddenly afraid of her. 'You stay away from me,' she hissed. 'You spooky little fr—'

She stopped herself just in time, but Lizzie knew what she'd been going to say. *Freak.* Then, without another word, Collette turned and ran from the tent.

'I'm sorry about my sister,' Dru said, patting Lizzie's shoulder in a way that made her shiver all over. 'She'll calm down. She's just upset.'

'You were just worried about Dru, weren't you?' Nora said to her. 'That's all it was. Just a wee fret. Got yourself all worked up.'

'I s'pose,' Lizzie said.

But deep inside, she knew it had been something more. And by the looks on their faces, the others clearly thought so too.

Early the next day, when Lizzie went to meet Madame Aurora, the first thing that greeted her was a low groan from inside the tent.

Pa used to sound like that, she thought to herself. After a night on the ale, he'd spend the morning nursing his aching head. It was best to be as quiet as you could around adults with hangovers – she'd learned *that* the hard way. Softly, she moved the curtain aside and looked in.

Madame Aurora was still wearing last night's make-up, and her eyes looked sunken and bloodshot.

Lizzie had caught her in the act of swigging from a bottle. Their eyes met.

'Morning!' Lizzie said brightly.

Madame Aurora hastily stowed the bottle under the table, which was covered with a spread of tarot cards. Before it vanished, Lizzie smelled the sharp, unmistakable tang of juniper. So, gin was Madame Aurora's tipple, was it?

'Draw that blasted curtain!' the fortune-teller snapped. 'Too much light angers the spirits!'

Lizzie knew that the spirits couldn't care less about the light, but understood that the bright sunshine was hurting Madame Aurora's throbbing head. She moved into the tent and let the curtain fall behind her. There was no sense in making an enemy of her new boss.

'Well, I'm stuck with you, so I'm going to make use of you,' Madame Aurora said. 'The punters will be lining up soon. When they do, I want you to keep your eyes and ears open.'

'Open for what?'

'Anything I can use!' the woman said, rubbing her eyes. 'Do I have to spell it out to you, girl?'

'To get a better connection with the spirits, and such?' Lizzie said carefully.

'Of course. The more I know about the client beforehand, the more I'll be … able to help them.'

Lizzie nodded slowly. So that was her game, was it? She had to hang around outside the tent listening to anything the waiting customers might let slip, such as their job or where they lived, or even what they were planning to ask about. Then she would quickly tell Madame Aurora, who could pretend that the 'spirits' had told her.

'I can do that, easy,' she boasted.

'You'd better,' Madame Aurora said darkly. 'There's another job you need to do. Do you know what *ambience* means?'

'It's a carriage they take sick people off in.'

'That's an *ambulance*, you stupid girl. *Ambience* means an atmosphere. Creating the proper mysterious ambience helps the client to believe.'

Lizzie nodded. That must be what all the occult flim-flam inside the tent was for. Just more show, more illusion.

'I need you to help create ambience, understand? If I say something like "Spirits, show your presence!", then you knock on the table, or mess about with the lamps. Make 'em go low and flickery, 'that's always a good one.'

'But don't get caught doing it,' Lizzie added.

Madame Aurora raised an eyebrow. Her make-up cracked like old plaster. 'You're catching on quick. You might be more useful than I thought. Here, sit down.' She stood, and made Lizzie sit down in her seat. Madame Aurora's breath stank of gin. 'Communing with the spirits takes a lot out of me,' she explained. 'I need to have a little nap now and again.'

'I bet you do,' Lizzie muttered.

'What was that?'

'Nothing.'

Madame Aurora began to unwrap the veils and shawls from around herself and drape them on Lizzie. They smelled like old sweat and gin. Lizzie wrinkled her nose but said nothing. This was the only job she had, and she mustn't lose it.

'While I'm resting, you'll have to cover for me,' Madame Aurora told her. 'Nobody will know it's not the real Madame Aurora under these wraps.'

'What am I meant to tell the punters?' Lizzie protested.

'Hold your horses a moment. There! Now you look the part. Can you do the voice?'

Lizzie coughed. 'You are troubled, dear,' she said, just as she had the night before.

'Close enough. Now, take my hand as if I was the client. That big line down the middle of my palm is the life line.'

'Got it.'

'Now run your middle finger down the life line. Gently!'

'Like this?'

'That's it.'

Lizzie frowned. 'That's funny.'

'What? What's going on?'

Lizzie said slowly, 'I can see something. Pictures in my head.'

'No, don't sound surprised! You're meant to be psychic! And remember to do the voice. Start with something like "the mists are parting…"'

'No, I really *can* see something,' Lizzie breathed.

An image was forming in her mind, right behind her eyes, as if a magic lantern was shining it there. It was blurred, like a watercolour left out in the rain, but she could still make it out.

A boy, making a pile of sticks to burn a broken doll on. And a little girl, crying.

'It's a dolly funeral,' Lizzie said.

Madame Aurora nearly jerked her hand right out of Lizzie's grip. 'What?'

'The doll's got broken, and the boy wants to burn it, but the girl don't want him to.'

'Amelia,' Madame Aurora whispered. 'How on earth...'

'Now there's something else.' Lizzie moved her finger further down Madame Aurora's life line. 'The picture's not quite so blurry this time. It's that girl again. But she's older. About sixteen? Wearing a bonnet. In a room, in a house. She's tying up a stack of letters with a big pink ribbon. And she's happy.'

'Happy,' Madame Aurora echoed.

Lizzie gulped and blushed a little. 'I think they're love letters.'

Madame Aurora opened her mouth and shut it again.

'Now she's on a stage, singing a song. The pictures are getting clearer! She's older now. She's trying her best, but they're booing her, poor thing.' Lizzie suddenly realized who it was in the visions. 'She looks like *you*!'

'What song?' Madame Aurora demanded. 'What

song, you little wretch?'

Lizzie strained to make it out. '"It was only a violet, plucked from my poor mother's grave…"'

Madame Aurora gasped. 'How dare you? You ungrateful, prying—'

'Now I can see you, just like you are today. It's not blurry at all. It's so clear, it's like looking right at you! And there's bright light… You've got your robes on, in this here tent, and you're talking to a bloke. A posh-looking gent—'

Then Lizzie stopped talking, because in her vision Madame Aurora was quite clearly stealing from her client. Lizzie watched her reach across, lift a pocketwatch from the client's jacket and slip it into her own. Then the vision vanished.

Madame Aurora snatched back her hand, and before Lizzie could say another word, she pulled her up by her shoulders, tore the veils and robes off her and shoved her out of the tent.

'Who in hell do you think you are, eh?' she screeched from the doorway. 'I'm the fortune-teller in this show, not you! You cheeky little upstart, I'll skin you alive!' Then she bent over, clutching her head and wincing. 'I'm going for a nap.'

'What about the clients?' Lizzie protested.

'Stuff the ruddy clients! And stuff you too. Get out of my sight! You're finished here, do you hear me? Finished!'

CHAPTER 7

Much later, after night had fallen, Lizzie made her way across the circus camp. Madame Aurora's angry words were still ringing in her ears.

The night air was chilly. Above the London rooftops the stars were out, brilliant as sequins against the black velvet sky. Lizzie thought of the zodiac signs she'd seen on the drapes in Madame Aurora's tent – a swirl of fantastic beasts and mythical figures.

'Load of rubbish,' she muttered. 'They're just stars. People shouldn't go making up shapes that ain't there.'

She knocked on the door of the Fitzgerald trailer, the largest of them all, and Malachy called from inside,

'Come in, Lizzie! I think we can squeeze in one more.'

Inside, the caravan was packed with mementos – battered top hats, old canes, brightly coloured juggling clubs. Even the walls were encrusted with handbills and pictures of past performances. Lizzie hesitated, wondering where on earth she could sit.

'Over here!' Nora called from the far end, where she sat cross-legged on the bed below the window. 'We'll be snug as sausages.'

Lizzie shuffled past Dru, Hari and Erin, who were crowded around a low table to play cards. Piles of peanuts were changing hands instead of money.

'Take off those batts before you climb on the bed,' Malachy warned her.

'He means your shoes,' Nora laughed, answering Lizzie's blank look. 'You'd better learn more circus cant if you're going to be part of this troupe!'

Lizzie pulled her shoes off and settled down next to Nora. The bed was covered with a rainbow-coloured patchwork quilt and heaped with cushions. A light rain began to rattle against the window, making Lizzie feel all the cosier in this private world – it would hurt to have to leave.

'Not much good me learning your ways if I'm

getting thrown out on me ear tomorrow,' she said.

Nora stared. 'Who told you that?'

'Madame Aurora, who'd you think?'

'Oh, don't let that woman scare you,' Nora said. 'It's just the gin talking. She's a devil for the gin, that one.'

'So I can stay? I don't have to go?'

Malachy looked up from his card game. 'Of course you can stay. Why wouldn't you? Here, Lizzie, you're as white as a sheet! What's this all about?'

The card game was instantly forgotten as they all crowded around her. Lizzie swallowed. 'I-I don't think I should say.'

'What did that old hag say to you?' Erin demanded.

'I didn't mean to do it!' Lizzie burst out. 'I just saw things! The moment I touched her stupid old life line!'

It all came pouring out. She told them everything that had happened in the fortune-teller's tent.

When she described the visions, Erin and Nora listened open-mouthed. Malachy paid close attention and Dru folded his arms and said nothing. But Hari...

Hari didn't even seem surprised.

'I think you have a gift, Lizzie,' he told her softly, once she'd finished.

'Garn! Get away!'

'In India, we have holy men who are supposed to have wonderful powers. They can levitate, read minds, and even walk on hot coals. Perhaps…'

Lizzie was having none of it. 'I'm not from ruddy India, I'm from Rat's Castle!'

'Sounds like you saw Aurora's life story,' Malachy said. 'Pretty miserable life too.'

'Lizzie saw her past,' Hari agreed. 'But I wonder… You say the visions become clearer the closer you came to the present day?'

'Yes.'

'So the blurrier a vision is, the further in the past it is. Tell me, then: was there a vision that was clearer than clear? Shining bright?'

'Yes! How did you know?'

'Just a guess,' Hari said. 'If you saw her past, maybe you saw her future too. That's how I'd expect it to look.'

Nora gripped her arm excitedly. 'The *future*? What did you see?'

'It was her, in the tent, like she is now. She had a punter in. She was stealing his watch.'

Dru gave a low whistle and Erin and Nora exchanged glances.

'I didn't mean to see it!' Lizzie protested. 'I couldn't

help it!'

Malachy rubbed his chin. 'Old Aurora, a thief? I wouldn't be surprised if that was true.'

That took Lizzie by surprise. 'Really?'

'Come on, have you seen how much gin she gets through? More than she could afford on a fortune-teller's wages, I bet.'

'She's a proper souse,' Erin said, nodding.

'Gets into barnies all the time, when she's been taking the drink,' said Nora. 'Remember the cat-fight she had with the Amazon Queen?'

'Savage, it was! Scratching and hair pulling! Rolling in the straw!'

'If Anita hadn't knocked her cold with that tent peg, she'd have murdered someone!' Nora laughed.

Lizzie didn't think it was funny. She'd made a dangerous enemy, she now realized. If a drunken Madame Aurora could attack the huge Amazon Queen, then what chance did a skinny young girl have? 'Forget it,' she mumbled. 'It must have been my imagination.'

'And when the rope broke, and I fell? Was that your imagination?' Dru said, speaking for the first time.

'She's got the second sight,' Erin said, totally sure. 'That proves it. Here. Do me next.'

Lizzie squirmed away from Erin's offered hand. 'I don't believe in none of that stuff.'

Dru shrugged. 'Seeing is believing.'

Lizzie had never believed in anything supernatural – she wasn't even afraid of ghosts, not like other children she knew. After all, Pa's fists were more scary than any ghost could be.

And now this.

'But this circus stuff ain't real,' she said desperately. 'It's all just a show for the punters.'

'Some of it is,' Malachy told her. 'But it's a big old world, Lizzie. There are a lot of strange things in it that you can't easily explain.'

'S'pose you'd know,' Lizzie said sullenly.

Malachy grinned. 'We've been to a lot of places, us circus folk. Seen things that would turn your hair white. You're going to have to open your mind if you're going to stay with us.'

It was a lot to take in. Lizzie looked down at her own open hands, wondering if she really did have the power to see into people's lives. Deep inside herself she suddenly believed that she did. Whether she liked it or not, there wasn't any other explanation. All through her life, she'd had premonitions. She'd dreamed of her mother's death, and her brother's, but she'd thought it was just coincidence – after all, people died all the time in Rat's Castle.

The only question now was what she should do with her powers. Well, they could help make money, for a start. If she could tell people about their past the way she had with Madame Aurora, they'd be more likely to part with their cash. She might even pick up on some forgotten happy times that the customers would be glad to be reminded of.

'Looking into the past is harmless enough, I reckon,' she said. 'But do you really think I can see into the future?'

'Like when you saw Aurora stealing?' Malachy rested his chin on his fist. 'That vision was clearer than the rest, wasn't it?'

'All bright and shiny.' Lizzie nodded.

'So if that *was* the future, then perhaps she hasn't stolen anything yet…' A faraway look came over Malachy. Then, suddenly, he leaped to his feet. 'Lizzie, I've got it. We can't change the past, but we *can* change the future.'

'What are you on about?'

'Maybe you've been given visions so that you can

stop bad things happening!'

'How?' Lizzie boggled.

'Think about it. If something bad hasn't happened yet, maybe it doesn't have to happen at all.'

'If you knew when and where a robbery was going to happen,' Hari added excitedly, 'you could get there first and stop it!'

'You could be a hero,' Erin said.

For once, Lizzie was completely lost for words.

The next morning, Lizzie was ready for work in double-quick time. She looked at herself in one of the carnival mirrors. Dressed in the dark formal clothes she'd borrowed, she looked like a mourner at her own funeral. She sighed. Time to go and face Madame Aurora's wrath.

But the moment she headed out across the green towards the fortune-teller's tent, she started to attract attention. A clown smiled through a beard of shaving foam and waved. Women whispered behind their hands and an old man covered in tattoos blew out a cloud of pipe smoke and nodded knowingly.

Lizzie picked up speed. That only pushed the excitement on the site up another notch. Now people were standing up, abandoning half-eaten breakfasts, stowing away borrowed newspapers. She heard someone call out: 'There she is!'

Lizzie spotted Nora's red hair and strode across to her.

'Morning!' Nora said with a smile that spoke volumes.

'Did you and Erin tell everyone about me having them visions?' Lizzie demanded.

'Oh, we might have let it slip,' Nora said breezily. 'Now would you look at that, you've got customers already.'

Lizzie spun round. People were heading directly for her now. A group of eight or nine circus folk quickly gathered around her, talking excitedly.

A lean, brown-skinned man stepped forward first. It was Zezete, the man she had met taking Akula the elephant for her bath. 'My nephew Hari tells me you have a gift,' he said.

'Hari too?' Lizzie rounded on Nora. 'So the whole lot of you have been telling tales about me around the camp, have you?'

'My dear girl, if it is true, then it is nothing to be ashamed of!' Zezete smiled at her warmly. 'Such gifts are given for a reason, always.'

Lizzie shuffled her feet. 'I don't want it.'

'Why ever not?'

Lizzie lowered her eyes. ''Cos I'll just get called a freak.'

'But we are all freaks at Fitzy's circus,' said Zezete with a wink. 'You will fit right in.'

She had to smile at that.

'So, madam, would you do me the honour of reading my palm?'

Lizzie took a deep breath. 'All right.'

His hand was warm in hers, and the gathered crowd looked on eagerly. She found the life line. It was deep, like a weathered canyon carved through rock. The moment she put her finger to the line, visions began to appear in her mind. She saw a blazing sun, men wearing turbans and women with brightly coloured cloth wrapped around them, and cows wandering down the middle of a busy road.

'I can see a town, but it's not in England. There's crowds of people, and cows in the street.'

'India,' Zezete said confidently.

Lizzie gasped at the colours she saw before her: red and blue banners, gleaming gold on temple roofs, bright powder paint exploding like bombs in the midst of a joyous festival.

'There's a celebration,' she said. 'People chucking paint about.'

'Yes, yes! Holi, the festival of colours. Excellent. Very good. Go on.'

'You're a little boy, and some old holy bloke is touching your head.'

'Swami Samarth,' Zezete told the onlookers delightedly. 'I was three! I had colic. My mother took me for a blessing.'

'Now you're eating a cake with loads of layers.'

Zezete groaned and licked his lips. 'Bebinca.'

Lizzie wondered how long it had been since Zezete had tasted any. The young boy in her vision was savouring every mouthful, and the vision was so intense that she could smell the sweetness of it. Her mouth began to water.

The vision vanished, replaced by another. Zezete was a man now, still eating bebinca. He smiled up at the beautiful woman who had brought it to him. Lizzie spoke the words she was saying:

'Happy birthday, my little squirrel.'

Zezete began to tremble over his whole body. He whispered something in Hindi that Lizzie couldn't understand. 'My Lakshmi,' he begged. 'Tell me more of her.'

But the vision had already faded. 'I can't,' Lizzie said helplessly.

'But you saw her! My wife… she always called me her little squirrel!' Zezete's face became solemn. 'I will pay. Whatever you ask. Just give me more.'

'Money won't help. I don't choose what I see. It just happens.'

Zezete closed his eyes. 'Very well. You must speak as you see.'

Lizzie tried to focus again. Suddenly, just as had happened with Aurora, she saw a clear vision.

'I see you, in your trailer, looking in your travelling trunk. You're fishing around by some old boots. A ring's on a chain round your neck. Now you're standing up, but the chain's got caught. The ring's fallen into the trunk.'

Zezete sprang to his feet, eyes wide. 'Thank you!' he said. Then, without warning, he kissed her on both cheeks before rushing off.

After that, everyone wanted their palm read. Lizzie had to make them all line up. She was in the middle of reading the palm of a Dutch acrobat called Erik when a shout of joy rang out from Zezete's caravan.

'So you're sure I don't have consumption?' Erik was asking.

'How could you go on to have grandchildren if you have consumption? I saw you with them. It was Christmas and you were an old man! The only thing wrong with you now is a spot of hay fever. 'Scuse me a moment.' She turned to see Zezete sprinting towards her. With both hands he was holding up a golden ring that caught the light.

'Her wedding ring,' he said through tears. 'I lost it weeks ago, when the circus was in Cambridge. I thought it was gone for ever.' Zezete grabbed Lizzie's arm and held it up as if she were a boxing champion. 'Listen, all of you!' he declared. 'This girl is *echt*, kosher, the genuine article! My mind-reading is only stagecraft, but she is a *bona fide* psychic! I have never seen the like!'

'What in hell is this?' screeched Madame Aurora's voice. The crowd parted, revealing the fortune-teller stumbling out of her tent. She came barrelling towards

Lizzie. 'Shove off, you lot!' she told the onlookers. 'This brat works for me, and don't you forget it!' As they dispersed, Aurora bent down low and whispered wetly in Lizzie's ear: 'Last chance. If you don't stop stealing my limelight, I'll get you fired … or worse.'

'Worse?'

Aurora grinned, showing yellow teeth. 'I can do magic too, you know. I can make nasty little girls disappear. Never to be seen again.'

CHAPTER 8

Lizzie barely slept at all that night. All day she'd worked hard in the mystic tent, eavesdropping on the customers and fiddling with the lamp like Madame Aurora wanted, while the murderous threat hung in the air between them.

'*Never to be seen again…*'

Lizzie shuddered and rolled over. Visions rose like smoke in her mind, keeping her from sleep. Aurora, grinning like a skull. A gleaming knife. The masked Phantom, laughing.

She woke up the next day, rolled groggily out of bed and went to join the Sullivans for breakfast. Erin snatched her porridge away when it looked like Lizzie was about to pass out into it.

'Shall I fetch a bucket of water and chuck it over you?' Erin suggested. 'Might wake you up.'

'My legs ache,' Lizzie moaned, rubbing her calf.

'That's because that old witch makes you stand in one place all day.' Nora said.

Mr Sullivan checked his watch. 'You'd better be getting off to work, Lizzie. She'll have your guts for garters if you're late.'

But when Lizzie arrived at the fortune-teller's tent, she found it empty. She hastily lit the lamp, set some incense burning and tidied up as best she could, hoping it would improve Aurora's mood if she found the place ready for her.

Ten more minutes passed. Still no sign of Aurora.

Lizzie poked her head out of the tent and saw the first of the day's customers waiting patiently in line. She bit her knuckles anxiously. It was bad for business to leave customers waiting. She could do the readings herself, of course, but Madame Aurora wouldn't like that, would she?

She paced back and forth, lit more incense, polished the crystal ball, straightened the tarot cards. Outside she heard someone mutter, 'We can't expect these circus folk to turn up on time, can we?' and polite laughter followed.

This was just confirming all their prejudices about circus people. Lizzie sneaked another peek outside. The queue had grown to seven or eight people now. The gentleman at the back was frowning and looking at his pocketwatch.

Lizzie's blood turned to ice on the spot. It was the man from her vision. And that was the very watch she'd seen Aurora steal!

Just at that moment, Madame Aurora barged into the tent, red-eyed and haggard. Ignoring Lizzie completely, she rummaged around under the table and came up empty-handed. 'Damnation,' she muttered. 'I was sure there was one more bottle... Right, Roxanna. Let the first customer in.'

Lizzie opened up the tent flap, feeling like she was trapped on a runaway train. Her vision was becoming a reality and there was nothing she could do to stop it.

'About time,' muttered a top-hatted gentleman who ducked past her first, wincing as he did so. 'You'd better be good!'

Lizzie couldn't possibly get away now. She stood,

her legs aching and her heart pounding, as Madame Aurora bluffed her way through the reading. 'You are troubled, dear…' she began.

Lizzie cringed as the hung-over fortune-teller mumbled her patter. It was a clumsy, half-hearted performance even by her usual standards.

The customer wasn't impressed, Lizzie could tell. She thought he might even demand his money back. She had to do something. Why had the man flinched in pain when he entered the tent? She glanced at his shoes. The left one was scuffed and worn down the side, as if he'd been favouring it. So, he had a bad leg. Maybe a war wound. She caught Aurora's eye and quickly mimed firing a gun, then slapped her leg.

'I see fighting in your past,' Aurora said instantly. 'A war wound, in the arm, *no*, in the leg. A brave soldier, who does not boast of his deeds…'

That made the man sit up and pay attention. *Nothing like flattery to win them over*, Lizzie thought sourly.

By the time he left the man was smiling, proud of himself. Lizzie had to get out. 'Shall I pop out and have a look over the others, then?'

'Of course!' Aurora snapped. 'You should have done that anyway.'

Outside, Lizzie glanced at the line of customers. Her stomach lurched to see the man with the watch was even closer to the front now. Some of the others must have grown tired of waiting and left.

It looked like her vision was about to come true. She had to tell someone. But if she left her post, Aurora would have her fired for sure. She'd be risking everything...

Lizzie made her mind up. She sprinted off to find Malachy and Nora. 'It's him,' she gasped when she found them. 'The gent with the watch! When he goes in that tent, she's going to nick it off him!'

'I knew you had second sight!' Nora said. 'Didn't I say?'

Lizzie's palms were clammy. She hopped up and down on the spot. 'But I dunno what to do!'

'I'll tell you what we're going to do,' said Malachy. 'We're going to catch her red-handed. Come on!'

The queue had shrunk even more. Now the gentleman with the watch was at the very front.

Malachy took up position outside the tent while Lizzie slipped inside. Aurora was in the middle of a reading. The pudding-faced old woman across from her was nodding at her every word. Aurora caught Lizzie's eye, and the look she gave her was pure poison. Lizzie gulped and threw a fistful of incense on the hot coals. Billowing clouds of smoke filled the tent.

'I see many grandchildren in your future,' Aurora went on. Behind her, the tent fabric twitched. Lizzie held her breath.

Nora came crawling in under the edge of the tent. The thick curtain of smoke almost hid her completely. Neither Aurora nor her client seemed to have noticed and Lizzie watched with her heart in her mouth as Nora quickly ducked behind the cabinet holding Aurora's mystic props. She let out the breath she'd been holding.

The old woman stood up to go, thanking Aurora again and again. Impatiently, Aurora ushered her out and beckoned the gentleman from Lizzie's vision in.

He sat down opposite her. 'I've never consulted a fortune-teller before,' he said anxiously.

'You have chosen wisely,' Madame Aurora said in her deep, husky voice. 'The spirits have a special message for you.'

'They … they do?'

'Roxanna!' She clapped her hands. 'Bring me the crystal!'

Lizzie's hands shook as she went to lift the heavy

crystal ball from its place in the mystic cabinet.

Nora's face peeped out from her hiding place, and she mouthed the words: *Is this him?*

Lizzie gave a quick nod and turned away. The crystal ball began to slip through her sweaty hands. She hastily set it on the table.

'I must enter a state of mystic trance,' Madame Aurora proclaimed.

'Gosh,' said the young man nervously. 'Right-o. Jolly good.'

Madame Aurora began to rock back and forth. She gave a long low groan like a sick horse, then rolled her eyes back into her head so that only the whites were showing. 'Spirits! I call to you! Come forth from your shadow realm!'

The gentleman sat stiffly in his seat, watching in amazement.

'Give some sign of your presence!' Aurora said through bared teeth.

Lizzie wasn't the least bit impressed. She had seen this routine a dozen times before.

Madame Aurora groaned louder. 'Spirits! Do not delay!'

Suddenly, Lizzie remembered she was supposed

to flicker the lamp at this bit. The gentleman almost jumped out of his seat when the light dimmed. 'Good lord,' he murmured.

'The spirits bid you welcome, O son of a noble line.' That was one of Aurora's old favourites. If the customer was high-born, they were flattered; if they were common, they were amazed to think their ancestors might have been blue-bloods. Either way, it was a winner.

The gentleman looked helplessly to Lizzie. 'What do I say?' he whispered.

'Lean forward,' Aurora boomed before Lizzie could speak. 'Gaze deep into the crystal. Only then can the message be given!'

He did as he was told, excitement all over his face. And the moment his waistcoat pocket came close enough, Aurora's hand moved like a striking snake. She wrapped her fingers around the watch, pulled it out and tucked it into her own pocket.

'Malachy!' Lizzie yelled at the top of her voice.

The poor gentleman jumped out of his chair with shock as Malachy pulled the tent flap back, letting in brilliant sunshine. A man was standing there in silhouette, arms folded. It was Fitzy himself!

'What's going on?' the customer cried, shielding his eyes.

'I'm afraid we're going to have to stop the reading,' Fitzy said.

'But … but … the spirits…' said the young man in total confusion.

'Never mind the spirits, my good sir,' said Fitzy, taking his arm. 'If you'd care to wait over here – *all* the way over here – that's it, so sorry for the inconvenience. I do hope you'll accept these free tickets for tomorrow's performance.' He ushered the man out of the tent and away through the circus, talking all the while.

Madame Aurora was on her feet, but Malachy stepped into the doorway, blocking her path. 'You're not going anywhere,' he warned.

'What's this all about, Malachy my love?' she said with a sickly smile.

Fitzy returned. 'I'm hoping it's nothing,' he said. 'Well, Lizzie?'

'She stole his watch,' Lizzie said boldly. 'It's in her pocket. I saw the whole thing!'

'You're a rotten little liar,' leered Aurora. 'You didn't see *nothing*!'

Right then, Nora sprang out from behind the cabinet and Madame Aurora gave a satisfying yelp of total surprise. Lizzie grinned at her friend's perfect sense of showmanship.

'I saw it too, Fitzy,' Nora said. 'Lizzie's telling the truth.'

With a weary sigh, Fitzy held out his hand. 'Come on, Aurora. Let's have it.'

Trembling, Aurora drew the watch out of her pocket. 'I couldn't help myself,' she stammered. 'It was the spirits... they drove me to do it.'

'The only spirit driving you is gin,' Fitzy said angrily. 'Nora, run and give the gentleman his watch back.'

'Right you are!'

'Tell him you found it on the ground and he must have dropped it. Enough of the public think we're thieves without us making it worse.'

Aurora fell on her knees and clutched at Fitzy's trousers. 'Don't call the rozzers, Fitz,' she begged. 'I can't go to prison, not at my age.'

'Save it for the beak. Malachy, go fetch Joey and Bungo.'

'Yes, Pop!' With a smart salute, Malachy darted off.

Aurora wailed and beat her fists on the dusty ground.

'Please! You don't 'ave to do this. I've been with you so long…'

Fitzy stood, hands on hips. 'So give me another option.'

'Let me go. I'll leave the circus and never come back, I swear!'

Fitzy pondered this. 'All right. But no second chances this time, Aurora. You're out for good.'

'Thank you, thank you!' Aurora struggled to her feet, tugged her mystic robes off and flung them on the ground. 'I'll just pop to my caravan, fetch a few things, then I'll be on my way—'

'You will leave *now*,' Fitzy commanded in a tone that made Lizzie shiver.

Malachy arrived, followed by two huge circus hands. One was bald with a walrus moustache, the other shaggy and bearded like a mountain man.

Fitzy nodded to Aurora and jerked his head towards the exit. Bungo and Joey instantly understood. They reached for Aurora, but she was already backing away from them, retreating toward the main gate like a vampire being driven into its crypt. Ignoring her shrieks, they grabbed her by the arms and began to drag her off.

'You did this to me!' Aurora screamed at the top of her voice. 'You! Lizzie Brown!' And she let fly a string of language so foul that Nora came up behind Lizzie and covered her ears.

'Get her off my site,' Fitzy said in disgust.

'You better sleep with one eye open, Lizzie Brown! 'Cos you'll never be safe in London again! I'll have you killed! I got connections! I'm *somebody*!'

'She's just a drunken old washout,' Nora said firmly.

But Lizzie's heart still thumped hard in her chest with every angry scream.

'You're dead meat!' came the fading cries. 'Dead meat…'

Fitzy tucked his thumbs through his braces and gave Lizzie a broad smile, as if nothing unusual had happened at all. 'Word travels fast in a circus,' he said. 'I've heard you've turned out to be a genuine psychic.'

'That's right,' Lizzie said. No sense in denying it *now*, was there?

Fitzy bent his knees, dropping down to Lizzie's level. 'I seem to find myself in need of a fortune-teller. I don't suppose, by any chance, you'd be interested in the position?'

Lizzie gawped. 'Who, me? I mean … yes! Yes,

I would!'

'That's that, then.' Fitzy smacked dust off his hands and peered up at the signage, gold letters on a midnight blue background. 'Oh dear. This won't do at all. "Madame Aurora", it says. Out of date now.'

'I'll get Dawson to paint it up fresh, Pop,' Malachy said.

Fitzy nodded. 'I want it done by noon today. Now, what to write…' With his finger he traced the arch the new words would follow, speaking his thoughts aloud. '"The Magnificent Lizzie Brown," he declared. 'There. How's that sound to you, Lizzie?'

'Fantastic,' Lizzie breathed. 'Absolutely blooming fantastic.'

CHAPTER 9

Lizzie hadn't realized taking Madame Aurora's job would mean taking her caravan too.

Pa Sullivan had pointed that out to her over tea. 'Now we don't mind having you bunk down with us in here,' he added, 'but that trailer's yours by right, and you need to lay your claim to it before some other fella does.'

So Lizzie, Erin, Nora and Dru had gone racing over to the black, peeling caravan in the far corner of the field. Someone had once daubed mystic symbols on the outside – a star, a moon and a cross-eyed cat – but the paint had almost completely flaked off. It smelled musty, like an old, unopened room.

'It's enormous!' Lizzie said, climbing inside.

'It's ancient, is what it is.' Nora looked around. 'Ugh. Look at the mess that old slattern's left it in. Even the spider webs are covered with dust!'

'I love it,' Lizzie said firmly. 'It's mine now. I'm going to look after it.'

Nora spat on her palms and rubbed them together. 'Well, you'll not be sleeping in it in this state, so you won't! Let's make a home of it.'

They made a bonfire of Aurora's old cushions and bedding, emptied out the cupboards and drawers, and borrowed a broom to sweep the dust out. Dru made a face when he found a grimy, old petticoat under the mattress. It went straight on the fire.

By sunset the caravan was an empty shell, smoked out with incense from the fortune-telling tent. A quick ask-around netted them enough fresh blankets and cushions to make it comfortable, just in time for the circus to strike camp.

For the rest of the evening, there was non-stop work. Tents had to be taken down, canvas folded away, poles dismantled, stalls packed up – and all of it had to be done the right way, with no carelessness or corner-cutting, or Fitzy would make you wish you'd never been born. There was no room for shirkers. Lizzie found plenty to do, carrying stacked-up stakes and looping up ropes into neat piles. It was exhausting, but it felt good to be pitching in with the rest of them.

Now the stars were out and the circus was on the move, heading across the sleeping city toward Tower Hamlets for their next stop. The long convoy of caravans and trailers moved slowly, with most of the circus folk sleeping while the drivers steered them through the night.

Lizzie, Erin, Nora and Dru sprawled happily on the cushions in Lizzie's jolting caravan, bone-weary but still too excited for sleep. The sound of Big Ben tolled out across the river and the rooftops.

'One in the morning!' Nora yawned. 'Even the owls have gone to bed.'

'Please, Lizzie,' Dru begged, holding his palm out, 'I want to know my future!'

Nora laughed. 'Are you still pestering?'

'Please!'

'Not a chance,' Lizzie said, smirking.

'Give it up, Dru,' said Erin.

Dru pouted. 'So unfair. All day she reads the palms

of *les étrangers*! But I ask her to read mine, as *un ami*, and she says no!'

'It's a lady's right to refuse,' Lizzie said primly.

'Perhaps you are afraid of what you may see.' Dru unbuttoned his shirt and leaned back on the pillows, as if he was trying to play the part of an Arab sheikh. '"What if he does not love me like I love him?" you are thinking. "I would die."' Dru put his hand theatrically to his forehead.

'You must have hit your head when you fell off that high wire,' Lizzie said, and doubled over with laughter.

Nora came to her rescue. 'Never mind him. Let's shinny up onto the roof. It's a grand night to watch shooting stars.'

'But the trailer's still movin'!'

'So?' Nora grinned impishly, then got up and opened the door. 'Afraid to fall?'

'Yes!'

Nora softened. 'I'll give you a hand up.'

Lizzie watched in amazement as Nora hoisted herself up out of sight in a few quick moves. She was so strong! Nora reached an arm down from the roof to take Lizzie's hand and she gripped Nora's hand tight. Below the caravan's single wooden step, the London street was rolling past faster than she liked. Then Nora pulled without warning, and Lizzie was lifted clean off her feet. She managed a sort of flailing scramble up the rear of the caravan, scuffing even more of the paint off as she went.

'See?' Nora said. 'Easy.'

'Blimey,' said Lizzie, settling down on the gently swaying roof. 'Good view from up here.'

The vast, open arch of the sky was thick with stars, like a daisy meadow. As they watched, a faint streak of light slid silently down the darkness.

'Make a wish,' Nora and Lizzie both said instantly. They looked at one another and burst out laughing.

The horse-drawn trailers clopped and creaked their slow, steady way through central London. In the streets, the night people were at large. A staggering man, his arm around his friend's shoulders, paused from belting out a sea shanty to cheer the passing caravans. Ragged girls screamed at one another from opposite street corners. A chestnut-seller, tapping the gas from a lamp to roast his wares, called out to anyone who might be listening: 'Nuts-oh, pipin' hot! Loverly nuts!'

It was like being in the audience of her very own circus, Lizzie thought from her high perch on the trailer. All of London was putting on a show, and she got to watch it.

'Better come back inside, Lizzie,' Nora said.

'In a minute,' Lizzie told her happily.

But then, to her horror, she saw a figure she knew. He staggered a few steps, stopped to prop himself against a lamppost and stare down at his feet, then staggered on. It was Pa, drunker than she'd ever seen him.

'Get down!' Lizzie shoved her friend down flat on the trailer roof.

'Eh?'

'He ain't seen us yet.'

But he had!

Pa looked up. His eyes went wide, then narrow. 'LizzEH!' he roared.

'Don't look at him!' Lizzie told Nora urgently. 'You mustn't look him in the eye. It sets him off!'

'You get down 'ere *now*, girl, do you hear me?' Pa bellowed.

The trailer was passing right by him now. Lizzie didn't want to look down into that horrible twisted face.

'That's never your old man?' Nora whispered.

Lizzie nodded.

The trailer shook as Pa's fist slammed into the side of it.

'Here, leave it out!' the driver at the front told him.

Pa sneered. 'Who you talkin' to, ya dirty gypsy scoundrel? Eh? C'mon an' take a swing at meh.' He hiccupped. A wave of froth washed out from his mouth and spattered on the pavement.

'Don't look at him,' Lizzie pleaded.

Pa began to jog alongside the trailer. 'Lizzeh!' he howled, as if she'd hurt him. 'You've let me down. Me own flesh and blood!'

Passers-by were starting to take an interest now, nudging one another and pointing. Lizzie wanted the ground to swallow her up – Pa was shouting even louder than the chestnut-seller was.

'I need yeh back! Come 'ome!'

Nora's arm was round Lizzie, hugging her tight. 'He'll not take you. Not while I'm here.'

Pa stopped, panting heavily, and the trailer began to leave him behind. 'I got nuffin' without you, girl! I'm penniless!' He spat the word out, and a lot of spit came with it. 'I got debts! I'll end up in the work'ouse … all cozza *yoo*…' Then fresh, ugly determination came over his face. His self-pity wasn't working. Anger took its place.

He came charging at her, his boots pounding the cobblestones.

'Selfish little wretch! I'll pull you down, I'll drag you 'ome, I will! By your HAIR!'

Lizzie clung tightly to Nora, who glared down at Pa. 'You will *not*!' she yelled down at him. 'Get out of here, you old devil!'

Pa spread his arms wide as he ran. 'I'm taking you 'ome…'

The next second, he went flying through the air like an acrobat, tripped by a loose paving stone. His huge chin smashed down on the stones and metallic objects shook out from his pockets and rolled free. He lay with his face in the gutter, groaning, brown mud spattered over his eyes and mouth, his hand still clutching like a hairy spider.

Lizzie stared in disbelief at the gleaming oddments that had been in her pa's pockets. Gold chains, watches and coins lay in the dirt. Passing street people descended on the treasures like pigeons upon breadcrumbs, and Pa was hidden behind a crowd.

'Your da's a thief?' Nora said.

'He always was,' Lizzie said, making a sour face.

'He's never nicked as much as that before, though. A few silk hankies, the odd watch maybe.' *He's gone up in the world since I left*, she thought bitterly.

Nora shook her head. 'Pockets full of other people's gold, and he still wants you to pay his debts. There's nerve.'

Lizzie nodded in agreement, but her thoughts were far away. With her out of the picture, Pa would have been desperate for money. Desperate enough to break into the bigger houses and rob rich people?

Maybe she'd dreamed of the Phantom because, deep down, she already knew who he was: her own flesh and blood? No. It couldn't be. Pa just wasn't clever enough to avoid getting caught. But she still shuddered at the thought.

'I ain't never going back to him,' she told Nora fiercely.

'You'll never have to,' Nora promised. 'You're one of us now.'

Lizzie felt close to tears, and not just from the shock of seeing Pa like that. His words had hurt. He'd called her a selfish wretch, in front of all those people. For all they knew, she was the bad one.

I did the right thing, she told herself. *He really would have dragged me off by my hair if he'd caught me. Thank God for Fitzy taking me in.*

The circus set up in a wide green park that lay like a blanket in the midst of London's East End.

Crowds were already beginning to gather before the tents were even up and there was a crush to get in on the opening day. The main tent was packed night after night, and the sideshows drew a waterfall of pennies and shillings.

'Always a good pitch, the East End,' Fitzy told her, surveying the sea of faces. 'Your poor hard-working man wants value for money, and that's what we'll give him, begod.'

Lizzie worked as hard as everyone else. The hard part wasn't seeing people's futures, she now realized. That part was easy. The hard part was telling the client the truth about what she saw. People didn't always like that.

'People don't go to a fortune-teller to be told the truth,' Malachy told her. 'They want you to tell them that everything's going to be all right.'

But Lizzie had made up her mind not to lie, even if it was difficult. An ounce of real help was worth a ton of comforting lies.

June came, bringing blistering heat and even more customers. Lizzie sweltered inside her airless little tent, the mystic robes feeling rough as sacking.

A round-faced man came in on an especially stifling day. Lizzie already had a headache. 'Now I'm not what you might call a believer,' he said, settling himself in the seat opposite Lizzie. 'All this psychic stuff is so much tommy-rot, if you ask me. But my wife believes it all lock, stock and barrel, so here I am.' He thrust out his hand, daring her to take it.

Lizzie smiled despite the sharp pain building up in her head. She took his hand and the pain suddenly trebled, searing through her skull like burning gunpowder.

The pain must have showed on her face. 'You needn't bother with the theatrics,' the man said smugly.

Right, Lizzie thought. *I'll show you.* She traced her finger down his life line. Visions began to appear, but it was hard to see them clearly through the clouds of pain in her head.

'I can see you walking along a beach, as a little

boy—' she began.

'I was hardly the only small boy to have gone to the seaside,' the client interrupted, and laughed at his own wit.

'You're crying… A crab's nipped your toe, and everyone's laughing.'

For a moment the man stopped chuckling and sat still. Then he scoffed. 'Happens to lots of children.'

Lizzie went on, describing what she saw. Her head was pounding now. The client refused to be impressed, no matter how many scenes Lizzie described. She tried to see clear details but it just hurt too much.

Suddenly a vision blazed in her mind, clear and bright as the sunrise, cutting through the fog of pain. 'I can see a tall house in an alley,' she said. 'Posh one too. There's a big bronze door knocker in the shape of a lion's head.'

She felt the man stiffen.

'You're coming out the door. Big bunch of keys in your hand. Looking left and right.'

'Well I'm blowed,' the client said. He seemed lost for words.

Lizzie shuddered. 'Something's close, something evil. It's like there's blood in the air.'

A nervous laugh. 'Back to the theatrics.'

'It's him!' Lizzie sucked air through her teeth.

'What?'

Lizzie bit her lip. *A man with a mask over his face. A sack over his shoulder. Creeping ever so quiet and slow, 'cos he don't want to be seen.* She strained to see more. She saw a church at the foot of the alley with a golden dragon perched on its tall spire. A voice was calling in the distance. It was the same noise she heard every night. '*Last show, last show…*' She let go of the man's hand and took a few deep breaths. 'Do you live in a tall house down an alley, sir?'

'No I don't,' said the man.

Lizzie frowned. Maybe her vision had been wrong. Or perhaps she hadn't understood it properly.

'But I *am* looking after a tall house while the owner is on holiday,' the man added. 'I watch over it during the daytime, then at night I make sure it's all locked up. Now will you tell me what on earth you're driving at?'

'I think you're going to be robbed…' Lizzie warned. She deepened her voice so he would take her seriously. 'By the Phantom himself!'

The man's cheeks puffed up like a frog's. He burst out laughing.

'It ain't funny!' Lizzie yelled.

'Oh, that sinks it!' he guffawed. 'Wait till I tell the wife! Psychics, indeed…' He wiped his eyes. 'Dear child, you've put on a cracking show for me, but you've pushed it a bit too far.'

Lizzie sat red-cheeked and fuming as the man explained that the police had offered special protection to all houses with valuables in them. The house's owner had asked the local police to keep an eye on his property – and hired him as a watchman for extra protection.

'So the one thing that definitely won't happen is a robbery! Not on my watch!' He was pink as a sliced ham from laughing now.

'I know what I saw,' Lizzie insisted.

'And by the Phantom, of all people! Tsk! Don't you know that the Phantom has been made up by the newspapers to thrill stupid readers?' He stood up, still laughing, and tossed Lizzie a ha'penny. 'You've earned it. What a little storyteller you are!' He left.

'Serve him ruddy well right if he did get robbed,' Lizzie muttered. She sat and stewed for a moment, then made her mind up and sprang out of the tent and went running after the man. His life could be in danger. He *had* to listen.

He was talking to a police constable up ahead. Neither of them had seen her. 'Something amusing, sir?' the constable was asking.

'Dark forebodings from a fortune-teller!' said the client. 'The Phantom himself is coming to rob the house I guard!'

They laughed together.

'I'd say you've been robbed already, sir, handing over your money to one of them lot,' the policeman said. 'Don't ever believe a word those circus folk tell you. They're cheats and liars. All of 'em.'

Lizzie turned round and walked away before she was seen. The constable's words burned in her ears. 'It ain't fair,' she whispered. 'I'm no liar! I just wanted to help.'

Despite the people who swirled around her, she felt very alone. She knew what she had seen. She might be the only person in the world who knew where the Phantom would strike next!

CHAPTER 10

The rest of the day couldn't go by fast enough for Lizzie. There was no chance to get away from the stream of clients, not even for a moment.

She had to tell someone about the Phantom. Someone who would listen.

Finally, she got her chance. Once the last of the spectators had been ushered out of the show tent, she met up with Malachy, Hari and Nora there. Dru and Erin cartwheeled through the air high above their heads, cramming in some last-minute trapeze practice with Erin understudying for Collette. Lizzie almost couldn't bear to look.

Hari studied her. 'You've had another vision,' he said.

Lizzie stared at him. 'How can you tell?'

'You're clenching your right hand. The one you use to do the readings with. You did that last time too.'

Lizzie felt uneasy. She hadn't known Hari very long, but it was alarming how easily her new friend could read her. 'Beats me why anyone would ever play cards against you!' she joked.

Once Dru and Erin had clambered down the rope ladders, sweaty and breathless from their practice session, everyone gathered in a ring. Malachy sat on top of a hay bale, like a king holding court. He nodded for Lizzie to start speaking.

'Right. This is going to sound barmy, but just listen, all right?'

She had their attention.

'I had a customer today, he watches over a posh house. I saw it in the vision. And I saw someone come along with a sack as if they was going to rob it.' She took a breath. 'It was the Phantom.'

'You saw the Phantom?' Erin leaned forward, excited. 'What's he look like?'

'Nobody knows,' Nora said scornfully. 'He wears

a mask, doesn't he?'

Erin looked to Lizzie. 'What's the mask look like, then?'

'It's horrible,' Lizzie said. 'Like a ghost, or a skull, sort of. Big black eyes. I tried to warn the man, but he laughed in my face!'

Excited chatter broke out. Nobody even questioned the truth of what she'd seen. She felt buoyed up by their faith in her, as if she'd taken a jump into the unknown, only to be caught by a safety net.

'The question we ought to be asking,' Malachy said after the babble had died down a bit, 'is why you had this vision in the first place?'

'So I could warn him,' Lizzie said immediately.

'But he didn't listen, did he?'

'Lay off! I did me best!'

'I know. But think. What if he wasn't the one who needs to act?'

Lizzie held up her hands. 'So who is meant to, then? Me?'

A hush fell upon the gathering. They all looked at one another. Were forces beyond their control setting some great hunt in motion, some adventure beyond anything they'd ever imagined?

'It stands to reason,' Malachy said quietly, 'that a power that can see the future would have known your client wouldn't listen. So if the vision wasn't meant for him, it must have been meant for you.'

The penny dropped. 'You reckon I've got this … this gift of mine so's I can stop crimes happening, don't you?'

'I honestly do, yes.' Malachy jumped down from his perch. 'And let's face it, you've already stopped one, haven't you?'

'Aurora,' Erin said.

Lizzie remembered Aurora's blood-chilling threats as she was dragged away. She hadn't just stopped a crime, she'd made an enemy. Now Malachy was pushing her to confront the Phantom, who was far more dangerous. All of a sudden, she felt sick.

'P'raps I should just forget all about it,' she said. 'It's a bit risky. I don't *have* to do anything, do I?'

'You can't be serious!' said Nora. 'What if you'd just let Aurora rob that man? You think she'd have stopped with him?'

'She'd have gone on stealing,' Dru agreed. 'And when she was finally caught, it wouldn't just be her who got the blame.'

'The public would have blamed the whole circus!' said Malachy.

Hari looked up. 'If you are the only one who can stop the Phantom, Lizzie, then you have a duty to do so.'

'Why does it have to be me, though?' Lizzie complained. 'Ain't it the police who are supposed to stop criminals?' But even as she spoke, she remembered what the passing bobby had said. 'I suppose the coppers are a waste of time,' she sighed. 'At least, that one I saw today was.'

'You saw a policeman on the site?' Malachy frowned.

'He spoke to my customer. "Don't ever believe a word those circus folk tell you," he said. Called us all cheats and liars.'

Eyes rolled and tongues tutted all around the circle.

'*Comme toujours,*' muttered Dru. 'The police do not like us, Lizzie. Whenever we come to town, we are the first to be blamed if there's a crime.'

'Heard it a thousand times,' sighed Nora. 'Thieving travellers, they think we are.'

'*Git out of it, you Irish tinkers!*' Erin cried in a mock Cockney voice.

'A policeman grabbed my ear once,' Hari said

gloomily. 'He warned me not to use my "Indian rope trick" to climb into windows and steal. I laughed. I told him such tricks are make-believe.' Hari pointed at a white scar on his cheek. 'He gave me this for talking back to him.'

'Safe to say we won't be going to the police,' Malachy said. 'Sorry, Lizzie. They're always like that where we're concerned.'

Lizzie rose to leave. If the police wouldn't help and the adults wouldn't act, then she'd just have to confront the Phantom herself. Once she'd figured out where to start, of course.

'So we'll have to be the ones who investigate.' Malachy touched her arm, stopping her in her tracks. 'You didn't think we'd let you do this alone, did you?'

Lizzie gawped. 'Seriously? You're all in? Every one of you?'

Nora, Erin, Hari and Dru all nodded and grinned. Malachy tipped an imaginary hat in Lizzie's direction. 'All for one, and one for all.'

'Fantastic!' Lizzie cheered. 'So … erm … how are we going to catch him, then?'

'The same way we caught Aurora,' Hari said. 'You recognized the gentleman and his watch, so you were able to act in time. We must look for something similar in this new vision.' He sat cross-legged, his eyes closed. Lizzie was sure he was building up a picture in his remarkable mind. 'Tell us *everything*,' he said. 'Take your mind back. Talk us through what you saw. Every detail.'

And that is exactly what Lizzie did. She described the tall house, the lion's-head door knocker, the narrow alley, the church with the huge spire and the flying golden dragon perched on top, and lastly, the stooped figure of the Phantom, clutching his sack.

Hari asked question after question in a low calm voice, like a hypnotist. 'How many windows?'

'Nine or ten.'

'Was the sky light or dark?'

'Sort of halfway.'

'Was the sack empty or full?'

'Empty.'

The questions went on until Lizzie's poor head ached with the effort of remembering. If Hari was growing frustrated, he didn't show it. Somehow, that boy was always calm. Malachy paced back and forth, while the others looked on tensely, waiting for the moment of truth.

'Did you hear anything?' Hari finally asked, trying a new tack.

'Yes!' Lizzie burst out. 'A voice, shouting out, "Last show, last show!"'

'But that's us!' Nora cried, shivering all over. 'That's this circus!'

'I've got goose pimples,' Erin said with a shudder.

Malachy snapped his fingers. 'That tells us when it's going to happen! The callers call the last show at eight o'clock every evening.'

'When the sky is half dark and half light,' Dru added.

'So now all we've got to do is work out *where* it's going to happen. Let's get to work, folks. We have a crime to stop!'

They all leaped up and began to rush from the tent, except for Hari. 'One moment,' he said, still cross-legged, holding up a hand.

'Yes?' asked Malachy.

'If we are going to start investigating together, I think we should have a name.'

'Brilliant idea!' Erin said. 'We should be … the Show Tent Irregulars!'

'I don't want to be an Irregular,' Lizzie said darkly.

'Sounds like someone whose tummy's playing up.'

'Dru Boisset and The Human Oddities?' Dru suggested cheekily. Lizzie cuffed him around the back of the head.

'It needs "gang" in the title. We should be the *something* gang,' mused Nora.

Hari brightened. 'I like that! The Something Gang. It has an air of mystery.' He drew a question mark in the sawdust with a finger. 'My calling card.'

'Too much flipping mystery,' said Malachy. 'No, I know what we should be. It's obvious. It's staring you all in the face.'

They all looked at him, challenging.

'Well?' Lizzie demanded.

'*The Penny Gaff Gang!*'

Lizzie had to agree it was perfect.

CHAPTER 11

The next day was Lizzie's day off. Most of the circus folk went into town when they had free time, the men to drink and the ladies to shop, but Lizzie had very different plans. It was her versus the Phantom now, even if the Phantom didn't know it yet.

Ever since Malachy had told her not to bother with the police, she'd turned the problem over and over in her mind. Malachy was wrong, she decided. She hadn't even *tried* talking to the police. Yes, her client had laughed with the constable, but maybe she could make a different police officer listen.

All she had to do was prove she was serious. Seeing

was believing. And if she could convince a policeman that she had powers, then they'd have to take her seriously, wouldn't they?

Lizzie ran through the narrow, winding Whitechapel streets, looking for a police station. Alarmed people sidestepped out of her way. A dog tethered outside a pub barked savagely at her.

The more she looked, the more confident she felt. Hadn't the police admitted they were baffled, anyway? They needed any help they could get to catch the Phantom. What did it matter if it came from a circus fortune-teller?

She finally found what she was looking for on Leman Street. Inside, the police station was gloomy and smelled strongly of carbolic soap and writing ink. A desk sergeant with bags under his eyes looked down at her.

'I'd like to help you with an investigation,' Lizzie said proudly.

'Sling your hook,' the sergeant said. 'We're not taking on any informants.'

Lizzie drew herself up to her full height. 'I'm not here to peach someone up! I've learned something what could be of importance! Some bloke's going to get robbed unless you stop it.'

A second officer entered, moustached and smart in his uniform, bringing two enamel mugs full of tea. He glanced at Lizzie as if she were something a cat had thrown up on the rug. 'What's this?'

'She says she's got *information*,' the sergeant said, accepting his tea.

'Has she, begod,' said the officer. 'Where's she come from, then?'

The sergeant's pale grey eyes were on Lizzie, who suddenly found she was having trouble speaking. 'Well?'

'I'm with Fitzy's Circus,' Lizzie said hesitantly. She was beginning to wish she hadn't come here.

'A circus brat!' The desk sergeant laughed. 'Come on then, love. Hand 'em over.'

'Hand what over?'

'The free tickets, of course.' He turned to his fellow officer. 'They try this once in a while. Give us free tickets to a show and hope we'll look the other way when one of their lot gets collared.'

The moustached policeman blew ripples in his tea. 'They'll stoop to anything, won't they?'

This wasn't going the way she'd planned at all. 'I'm

the fortune-teller!' she yelled. 'But I'm not a scammer, I really can see the future!'

The sergeant rolled his eyes. 'Pull the other one.'

'The Phantom's going to do another robbery, and you lot need to stop it. If you don't help, then me and my friends are going to have to stop him ourselves!'

'I think this has gone on long enough,' said the moustached officer, with a nasty edge in his voice. He walked around from behind the desk and loomed over Lizzie, who backed away. He grabbed her ear in a painful pinch. 'You and your raggedy little friends should keep your noses out of grown-ups' business, understand?'

'Ow! Getcher hands off me!'

He was dragging her to the door. 'Better stay on your site from now on, if you know what's good for you. We don't like your sort.'

'And if you don't, we've got some nice cells you can come and kip in,' the desk sergeant added with a yawn. 'If I see any of you circus brats out on the streets playing your tricks, getting in honest people's way, I'll lock you up for begging. Quick as spit.' The policeman bent down and whispered, 'Didn't see *that* coming, did you, fortune-teller?'

Lizzie was shoved through the doors and found herself back on the pavement, rubbing her sore ear and scowling. *Even if they didn't believe me, they didn't have to be rotten about it!*

She could still hear the desk sergeant talking indoors. 'Better see about cancelling Overton's leave. When the flaming circus is in town, petty crime goes through the roof so we'll need all hands.'

'He won't like it.'

'He can lump it. He's needed. Circus people! They're worse than the gypsies, that lot.'

Lizzie marched off down the street, her head full of angry thoughts. *I won't be telling Malachy about this. I know exactly what he'd say: 'Didn't I warn you not to bother with the police, Lizzie? They'll lock you up soon as look at you.'*

Well, she wasn't going to go back to Malachy and the rest of the Penny Gaff Gang empty-handed. If the police wouldn't help her, she'd help herself.

What had Hari said? They knew *when* the robbery would happen. They just needed to know *where*. She thought back over what she'd seen in her vision. Tall, narrow houses were ten a penny in the East End. So were alleyways. But a church with a golden dragon on the spire? That ought to stand out like a clown at a funeral…

'I'm on the hunt for a golden dragon!' she said to herself, breaking into a run.

Dodging out of the way of ladies with parasols and gentlemen with canes, she threaded her way through the twisting East End streets. She had to look up often, which meant bumping into people and tripping over cobblestones, but there was no other way to look for a golden dragon over the rooftops.

She could still see it clearly in her mind. It had a wavy body, like a sea serpent on an old-fashioned map. *Here be dragons*, she thought. Except there weren't any dragons anywhere she looked. She passed ironmongers and pubs and sawdust-floored butcher's shops that reeked in the heat. There were churches, plenty of those. She even passed St Mary's Chapel with its high white walls, giving its name to the district. But not one had a golden dragon on the spire.

A nanny went by, pushing a pram. The police had warned Lizzie not to bother anyone in the street. She looked around. No police anywhere in sight.

''Scuse me?'

'Hello, petal!' Her face shone like a freckly sun.

'Are you lost?'

'I need to find a golden dragon. Have you seen one?'

'I'm terribly sorry, but no. No golden dragons, pixies or prancing unicorns neither.' She giggled. 'Good luck!'

'Thanks!' Lizzie shot off down the street, hoping the next face she met would be just as friendly.

But though many of the East End folk were happy to give her the time of day, none of them could point her to a golden dragon. Lizzie was growing uneasy. The more she ran from street to street, the more paranoid she felt. Any moment now, Pa might lurch out from behind a door, full of beer and fury. Madame Aurora could swoop like a harpy and clutch at her.

Or the police might grab her. She must have spoken to over a dozen people, she realized with a sickly feeling. That was surely enough to get her arrested for begging.

I want to go home. Back to my caravan. Stuff the Phantom. But just as she was about to turn around, a sudden tingle in her palms stopped her. It felt like a nudge. 'Maybe just one more, then,' she whispered to herself. 'One more can't hurt.'

Her feet were aching. A woman in a back alley was sweeping dust out of her house in great clouds and squinted at her as she came close. The man lying in the gutter opposite gave her a wave and a drunken grin. His hat was missing its top.

'Golden dragon?' the woman said as if Lizzie had asked for the moon on a stick. 'Get on out of it.'

''Ere!' called the drunkard. 'I can show yeh! Golden dragons, is it? I see one every day.'

'Pink elephants is what he sees.' The door slammed.

Lizzie helped the drunk to his feet. 'Follow me!' he burped, then took off through the streets like a hot air balloon come loose from its tether. Lizzie almost ran into him when he stopped to think.

'Are we there?' she asked. She couldn't see the spire.

Deep creases appeared on his brow. Then he held his finger up. 'This way!' With a huge stride, he fell over.

Lizzie helped him up again, wishing there weren't so many people watching her. This was taking too long and attracting too much attention. But she continued to follow him from street to street, glancing over her shoulder, wondering how much time she had left. The drunk repeated 'golden dragon, golden dragon' in a sing-song voice. Perhaps he was mad. Perhaps she was wasting her time.

'Hurry up!' she begged.

'Madam,' he told her with great dignity, adjusting

his hat, 'the game is afoot!' They rounded a corner, and his arm suddenly flung out. 'Here 'tis! Just like I told yeh!'

Lizzie covered her face with her hand. He was pointing at a pub. The sign over the door showed a rearing yellow dragon with a barbed tail. She read the name aloud: 'The Golden Dragon.'

'So,' the drunk said, grabbing her arm, 'have you got a penny for me?'

She shook him off. His angry yells followed her as she stomped back down the street, picking up speed. *Nothing for it but to go back to the circus. Wasted a whole day. I feel like a proper 'nana!* But at the end of the street, she stopped dead. The church in front of her looked familiar. Her gaze moved up the elegant stonework, up the long, narrow spire, all the way up to the weathervane at the very top.

There it was, glinting in the sunlight – the golden dragon!

Lizzie stopped a passer-by. 'Please, sir, what church is that?'

'Saint Mary's-le-Bow.'

Now I can find my way back. I'm not losing this place again!

The alley had to be close by. Sure enough, she quickly found it, snaking around the back of the church.

She felt a queer thrill as she saw the house, in the plain light of day, exactly as it was in her vision. She wanted to go up and touch it, to prove it was real, but she didn't dare.

'He's coming,' she whispered to herself. 'P'raps he don't even know it yet. P'raps he's still choosing the house he wants to rob. But *I* know. And I'll be ready for him!'

Once she was back at the circus, though, she found she had nothing to do but wait. All of her friends were busy with their acts. With no work to do and nobody she could talk to, the afternoon passed slow and thick as molasses. She lay in her stifling caravan with the door and window open and listened to the oohs and aahs coming from the show tent.

Finally, the roar of applause told her that the afternoon show was over at last. The whole gang was soon crammed into Lizzie's caravan, eagerly listening to her story.

'We need a plan.' Malachy said, leaning forward from a corner full of shadows. 'I say we all get down to the house and find somewhere to hide, then once the Phantom shows his face – well, his mask – then we jump him.'

'We can't go,' Erin and Nora said together.

Malachy sighed. 'Oh, right. You missed it, Lizzie. My dad wasn't happy with the bullwhip routine.'

'She messed it up!' Nora jabbed a thumb at her sister. 'Came too close.'

'By a whisker!'

'Nearly clipped my head off, she did. So now we've *both* got to practise.'

'I made it look like I meant to do it!' Erin protested. 'Anyway, the audience loved it, so there.'

'I cannot come either,' Hari said, with sad eyes. 'My girls are in the show tonight. The elephants need me. If I am not there, they will fret.'

Lizzie felt like her chance was slipping away. *This is never going to work. They're all so busy. Why did I even bother?*

Dru stretched like a cat. 'I am in the show too, but on last. I will come, so long as I can be back for ten o' clock.' It was as if he was talking about going for a picnic. 'I think it will be *amusant*.'

'You, me and Lizzie.' Malachy grinned. 'Should be enough to catch a Phantom.'

Outside, in the humid evening air, they heard a nearby clock strike six. They agreed to meet up in an hour, so as to be in Cheapside in plenty of time to set up watch.

'Remember, the cry for the last show is at eight,' Malachy told them. 'That's when the Phantom arrives and we spring the trap.'

Malachy and Dru went to the tea tent to grab an early dinner, but Lizzie – for once – couldn't face eating a mouthful. Excitement had tied her stomach in a tight knot.

It was time for the hunt to begin, and this time the criminal was the prey.

CHAPTER 12

Lizzie glanced back over her shoulder. She caught a last glimpse of the tops of the circus tents, then the streets swallowed them up.

'Would you like to hold my hand?' Dru teased.

'Garn!' Lizzie waved him away. But even with Dru walking on one side and Malachy hurrying along with his stick on the other, she still felt nervous. It must have shown on her face.

She caught the eye of a stubble-faced man who glared back at her, and she quickly looked away. Was he following them? She put on a burst of speed to leave him behind.

'Hold up,' Malachy gasped. His club foot was slowing him down.

'I don't like being out here,' Lizzie admitted. 'I keep thinking I see … people.'

'Worried about Aurora? She won't lay a finger on you. We won't let her, will we, Dru?'

Dru cracked his knuckles. 'I can take her down if I have to. Don't worry.'

But Lizzie couldn't shake the cold blanket of fear that had settled over her shoulders. Pa might rough her up a bit, but he needed her alive. Aurora had promised to kill her. 'You're dead meat,' Aurora had said, and whatever else she might have lied about, Lizzie was certain she meant every word of that threat.

'We've got worse than Aurora to deal with, if the Phantom does show up,' she said. 'He's a nasty piece of work.'

'If we're going to get cold feet, then we shouldn't have come!' Malachy snapped. Then, seeing the look of dismay on Lizzie's face, he added, 'You're right, though. He did batter that one bloke half to death. We need to be careful.'

They turned into Leman Street and passed the police station Lizzie had been thrown out of. An officer was standing outside, but Lizzie didn't recognize him. They kept up a brisk walk until they were far past.

'He might not be so keen to batter us, though, might he? After all, we are just kids…' Lizzie's voice trailed away.

Dru snorted. 'This Phantom is a criminal. If we get in his way, he'll punish us. So we watch out for one another, *oui*?'

Not another word passed between them as Lizzie led them down street after street, until at last they stood at the end of the alleyway.

Lizzie pointed out the tall house with the lion's head knocker, feeling strangely like she was unveiling a monument. 'There it is!'

The house stood by itself, with little alleyways down each side. Lizzie guessed there was a yard at the back too.

'Looks posh all right,' Malachy said, casually leaning against a wall and trying not to look out of place. 'Just the Phantom's cup of tea.'

'What's the plan?' Lizzie's mouth was dry.

Dru shaded his eyes and looked up. 'Climb up the house. Watch from the rooftop until the Phantom goes in. Then we climb down, hold the doors shut, call for help, and … *presto!* Caught like a rat in a trap inside the house, yes?'

'Rooftop? Do I look like a flippin' monkey? I can't get up there! Why can't we just hide in the alley?'

'Three children lurking in an alley will attract attention.' Dru's eyes flashed with amused pride. 'Besides, these houses are as easy to climb as apple trees. You see all the stonework, those ledges, the way the windowsills stick out?'

Lizzie gulped. 'It's a bit high up…'

'Trust me,' said Dru.

He wasn't joking now, she could tell. She nodded. 'All right,' she whispered.

'Right. You two are on the roof. I'll keep lookout from the end of the street and move in once I see the Phantom, because there's no way I'm going up there with you.' Malachy turned on his heel and began to limp down the alley, leaning hard on his stick. Lizzie heard him mutter, '…be lucky to manage an apple tree with this rotten foot.'

Dru didn't hesitate. He darted into the alley beside the house, then once he was out of sight he dug his fingers into the crevices between the corner stones and began to climb.

'Do as I do,' he told Lizzie, 'and don't look down.'

'What if I fall?'

'I won't let you.'

Lizzie took a deep breath. She copied Dru's climb, matching his handholds and footholds. Spiderlike, Dru clambered up and past the first-floor windowsills and edged around to get a grip on a sturdy black drainpipe. He made it look as easy as breathing. There seemed to be a power in his hands and feet that defied gravity.

Lizzie wasn't finding it so easy. There was no safety net here, no rope to catch. Only the hard cobblestones below.

Dru pulled himself up and over the edge of the roof. The guttering looked about to snap under his weight, but it held. Once he was secure, he reached out a hand for Lizzie to take. 'Almost there! You are doing well. *Fantastique!*'

She puffed and gasped as she grabbed the guttering with one hand and clung to Dru's hand with the other. With amazing strength, he lifted her up and over the edge. Her feet dangled in space for a moment, then her weight settled on the warm roof tiles. She clung on, not wanting to move again, ever.

I made it.

They both crouched, breathing hard. Dru grinned at her. 'There. Was that so bad?'

Lizzie glanced down into the alley. Malachy sidestepped into a narrow alleyway. From the shadows he gave Lizzie a thumbs-up, and she silently returned it.

They lurked in their hiding places, alert for anything that might happen. Time ticked slowly by. At last there was movement. Like a figure emerging from a Swiss clock, the round-faced man Lizzie had met before appeared at the front door – the caretaker.

'There he is!' she whispered to Dru. His body pressed against hers as he peered over her shoulder.

Lizzie noticed the huge bunch of keys dangling at the man's wrist. No wonder he was confident the house wouldn't be robbed if it had so many locked doors. The man began a careful circuit of the outside of the house. First he checked the iron grilles that protected the lower windows, making sure the locks on each were secure. Then he walked down the side towards the rear of the house, vanishing from sight. *He must be checking the back door*, Lizzie thought.

'Get back from the edge!' Dru said.

Lizzie leaned back against the sloping roof. She

heard footsteps in the side alley below.

'He was checking the windows,' Dru explained in a whisper. 'If he looks up and sees us – *boum!* All over!'

They waited, hearts pounding, until Lizzie heard the footsteps move away again. She heard the caretaker fasten a lock, then another, and then yet another. She risked a peek, craning her head round to look down. The man looked right up at her hiding place and she whipped her head back again.

A moment passed. A bead of sweat ran down Lizzie's spine. Then she heard the man chuckle to himself. 'Just pigeons,' he said. He was moving away now, walking down the alley away from them, out of sight. Malachy gave an all clear wave.

The caretaker's heading home, Lizzie thought. *Home to his wife, who believes in all that supernatural nonsense. Funny old world, innit? A week ago, I never believed in none of it myself.*

She suddenly wondered, with a cold sick jolt of horror, if the round-faced man would make it home to that wife of his tonight. She was sure the Phantom had been carrying a bunch of keys just like his in her vision.

The Phantom must have chosen this house well in advance. And he needed the keys to get inside. So, unless the man was in cahoots with the Phantom, he was going to lose those keys very soon … and probably a lot of blood too. Just like that poor man in Spitalfields.

The moment the hour struck eight, Lizzie saw a movement from the end of the alley. A man was coming out of a tiny side street, little more than a gap between buildings. She elbowed Dru.

Steadily the figure crept towards the tall house. Every detail of the vision was coming to life in front of her. Far off in the distance, the circus callers shouted out, 'Last show!' The figure was glancing left and right, cautious as a stalking fox. A sack was slung over his shoulder, he held a black cane in his hand, and his face…

He looked in her direction.

He had no face.

Lizzie was staring right into the ghoulish mask of the Phantom! It looked like a screaming skull, but battered and yellowed with age.

'Can he see us?' she whispered to Dru.

'Let's hope not!'

Lizzie stayed stock-still, hardly even daring to breathe, until the Phantom moved on. This was as far as her vision had gone. Whatever happened next was uncharted territory.

The Phantom drew a bunch of keys from a pocket. That didn't make sense. How could he have taken them from the caretaker so quickly? The watchman had left in the other direction…

The Phantom slipped down the little side alley that led round the back of the house, disappearing from view.

'He's heading for the back door.' Dru began to clamber across the roof towards the rear. 'Follow me. And be careful!'

Lizzie ground her teeth. Climbing on this sloping roof wasn't easy. With every movement, tiles threatened to break loose.

She and Dru made their way across until they could see down into the back yard. Dru sat straddling the ridge at the top of the roof.

'It's easier to balance up here,' he offered.

Lizzie didn't fancy it. She peered over the edge and saw the Phantom standing at the back door. He was selecting one key from the bunch, muttering to himself. Lizzie strained to hear, but she couldn't make out a word.

She needed a better view. Maybe if she leaned over

a bit more… She shifted her weight, and suddenly she was sliding, her foot skidding away as a tile broke loose.

Dru lunged. He caught her dress at the shoulder and grabbed a fistful of fabric. It yanked up painfully under her arm as the tile skittered down the roof. Lizzie prayed it would land in the gutter.

It didn't. It fell and exploded in the alleyway and a startled yell came from below. The Phantom had heard.

Dru was staring down at Lizzie, his face contorted in despair. 'Get down there!' he hissed. '*Arrêtez-lui!* Stop him!'

'HOW?'

'Down the drainpipe, *vite*!'

Lizzie climbed over the edge and gripped the drainpipe with both hands. She managed a controlled, skidding descent that was a lot faster than the climb up. The Phantom was turning this way and that in the yard. Then he saw the shattered remains of the roof slate, turned on his heel and ran, heading for the other side passage where Malachy would be standing guard.

'Get him!' Lizzie shrieked at the top of her voice. She dropped down the last few feet and ran across the yard, past the back door where the keys were still in the door, and came up behind the Phantom.

He was advancing on Malachy, who was bravely standing his ground. The Phantom thwacked the black cane into his open hand, and Lizzie thought of the man he'd beaten almost to death.

'Drop it!' Malachy warned, though his voice shook.

For the first time, Lizzie heard the Phantom's voice. 'Move,' he grated. 'Or I'll split your skull.' He spoke in a deep, hoarse whisper. *He's putting it on*, Lizzie knew instantly.

'You think a cripple can't fight?' Malachy raised his own walking stick, brandishing it like a war club. 'Come on!'

In answer, the Phantom gripped the cane with both hands and raised it above his head. He didn't know Lizzie was there behind him. But if she didn't do something, he'd smash Malachy into a broken and bloody pulp. She clenched her fists and got ready to run at him.

Then, to her amazement – and the Phantom's – something snatched the cane out of his hands. From *above*.

Dru was there, his legs braced between the walls of the passageway, holding him suspended in a chimney-climb. Lizzie looked on in awe as he casually tossed the cane from one hand to the other, his spread legs holding him in place.

'And now,' Dru said, 'for that mask, eh?' The cane lashed out, striking at the Phantom's face.

It was too much for the Phantom. He ducked out of the way of the striking cane, pushed past Malachy and ran off in a blind panic.

Dru dropped nimbly to the ground. 'He's getting away! Come on!'

The three of them set off in noisy pursuit, Malachy lagging behind. The Phantom was already halfway down the street, running as fast as he could. He tugged the mask off his face, flung it back over his shoulder and vanished round the corner.

As Lizzie sprinted after him, she heard the clatter of hooves and the sound of carriage wheels beginning to turn. He must have had his own transport waiting, she realized. There was no hope of catching him now. *We were so close, so flaming close!*

Dru reached the mask and snatched it up. 'We have this much of him,' he sighed. 'At least, that is— Lizzie!'

'Eh?'

'*Les flics!* The police!'

Lizzie spun round. Four uniformed policemen were

sprinting towards them from the other end of the street, truncheons in their hands. *They must've heard all the shouting!*

'Get him!' she screamed. 'There's still time!'

The policemen charged straight past her. But Lizzie's delight changed to horror as she saw them grab Dru by the arms. He fought, kicking and yelling in French, but they quickly had him on the floor.

'What are you doing?' she howled. 'That's not the Phantom!'

'It's him all right,' one of the policemen grunted. 'Caught him with the mask in his hand!'

'And we'll have that off you too,' another one said, wrenching the cane out of Dru's grip. 'It's still got that poor sod's blood on the tip, see?'

The next ten minutes passed in a horrible blur. No matter how many times Lizzie and Malachy protested that the wrong person had been arrested, they were ignored. The police found the back door of the house open and retrieved the keys, congratulating themselves on this new piece of 'evidence'.

A crowd was beginning to gather and rumours were flying fast. The Phantom had been caught red-handed. He was a circus acrobat – so obvious! How else had he been able to clamber into all those houses unseen? And he wasn't even English. Well, you never could trust a foreigner, could you?

In the end, there were so many people filling the alley that Lizzie could no longer see Dru. All she saw were the policemen's helmets moving through the crowds as he was dragged away.

'Where are they taking him?' she screamed.

'Newgate,' said Malachy, pale and shocked.

Lizzie gasped. Like any Londoner, she knew the name. It was the harshest prison London had ever known.

CHAPTER 13

There were no smiles among the circus folk gathered in the show tent this morning. The Amazon Queen stood grim-faced; Mario the giant looked as though he hadn't slept, and even the clowns looked down at the ground and kicked at the dirt.

Lizzie could hardly bear to look at Dru's family. His father had his arm around Mme Boisset, who had red eyes from crying. His sister Collette hung her head and clasped her hands like a funerary angel.

'As you all know,' said Fitzy, 'today's rehearsals have been postponed. I've called this meeting to discuss the reason why.'

A few knowing eyes turned to Lizzie for a moment, then quickly looked away.

Why did that stupid roof tile have to give way? She'd never be able to forget the sharp *crash* as it shattered. It was like she'd been trusted with the heart of the whole circus and she'd smashed it into a million pieces. Nobody had had a kind word for her this morning, except for what was left of the Penny Gaff Gang.

Malachy, who was standing beside his father, gave Lizzie a look that said *it's going to be all right*. But then Collette glared at her with accusing hate, and she had to close her own eyes.

'I'm afraid the rumours you may have heard are true,' Fitzy went on. 'Dru Boisset has been arrested and charged with multiple burglaries. They think he's the Phantom.'

Murmuring broke out.

'They can't do that!' someone yelled.

'He's only a boy!' cried Anita.

Fitzy gestured for calm. 'Please! You will all get the chance to speak.'

'Ruddy coppers,' one of the clowns said, and spat on the ground.

Carefully, without laying blame, Fitzy explained

what had happened. He already knew the whole story: Lizzie and Malachy had gone straight to him the night before. Lizzie winced when he mentioned the vision she'd had. *I wish I didn't have this stupid second sight. All it's brought me is trouble.*

'The police cannot be persuaded that our Dru is not the notorious Phantom,' Fitzy finished. 'Being in possession of the cane and the mask was enough evidence to convince them of his guilt. The back door of a nearby house was also left open, with the keys in it, and a witness says he saw Dru jumping from roof to roof like Spring-heeled Jack.'

'He is no thief!' exploded Pierre, Dru's father.

'We know. Dru did not steal anything, and nobody is suggesting that he did.'

'The papers are doing more than suggesting it!' bellowed Mario, to mutters of agreement.

'The papers are not judge and jury, even if they like to think they are,' Fitzy said, with frosty calm. 'Let's not beat about the bush, my friends. This is a bad turn of events. But it could be a good deal worse. We will make sure Dru gets all the help we can provide, and in the meantime, let's remember we still have a circus to run.'

Lizzie felt sick to her heart. Dru had gone with her to catch the Phantom. But the papers didn't care about the truth – they just wanted to give the public the story they craved.

'We all know why they've arrested Dru!' It was the Amazon Queen, and she was furious. 'The rozzers hate us, Fitz. They've always hated us, and the magistrates and aldermen hate us too. You've 'eard the names they call us!'

'Of course I've heard!' Fitzy's sudden anger broke out, hushing them all. 'You think I haven't been called those names too, ever since I was Malachy's age? "Circus scum!" "Thieves and vagabonds!" From the very same people I have to smile and bow to every night!'

There was a hubbub of agreement. Lizzie realized, with some relief, that the circus folk were even angrier with the police than they were with her.

'We all know how it is,' Fitz went on. 'Whatever crimes they can't solve, they pin on us. Nothing ever sticks, of course, because it doesn't have to. They blame us, we move on to the next town, and the whole business starts over. But this time, they've made something stick. This time they've got a suspect, caught at the scene, and they're going to milk it for all it's worth.'

'And whose fault is that?' Dru's father pointed straight at Lizzie. 'Who got my boy into this trouble, eh? Who talked him into this stupid game and got him arrested?' He looked around for support. 'Who filled his head with talk of visions and told him he could be a hero? Well? Shall I spell it out?'

'Steady, Pierre,' said Mario, laying a hand on his shoulder. But Pierre shrugged it off. Everyone was looking right at Lizzie now and not many of the faces were friendly.

'It should be her in that prison, and not him!' sobbed Dru's mother. 'And as for your son, Fitz—'

'That's enough!' Fitzy said. 'It's not Lizzie's fault that Dru's in prison. The coppers are to blame, and you both know it!'

'Dru should never have been there,' Collette said. 'If that weird girl hadn't lured him along, he'd be safe.'

'If Dru hadn't been there, Malachy would be dead now,' Fitz shot back at her. 'Your brother saved my son from being beaten to death. He *is* a hero, so far as I'm concerned!'

Collette had no answer to that.

'Now, tempers are running high and that's to be expected. But let's not start turning on our own. If we don't stick together, then that lot out there will be only too happy to tear us apart.'

A few heartfelt 'Hear! Hear!'s were the response.

Lizzie felt her eyes beginning to brim with tears, not from sadness but from the frustration and guilt boiling up inside her. Whatever Fitzy might say, however grateful he might be for Dru saving Malachy's life, all this was her doing. She couldn't run away from that.

I'm going to set things right again, so help me. Dru's innocent. I can't let him suffer because of me!

Zezete noticed that Lizzie was crying and he put his arm around her to show he was on her side, then spoke up. 'There must be other witnesses, surely. So where are they? Did nobody see the real Phantom flee the scene?'

'We can only hope someone comes forward,' said Fitzy. 'But even if they do, the police don't want to listen. Dru makes the perfect scapegoat. And the first robbery occurred around about the time we arrived in London, which doesn't help matters.'

'So what are you going to do?' Pierre demanded.

Fitzy rolled up his sleeves. 'Above all, the show must go on. Tomorrow, we move to Victoria Park. You all know how important that is. It's our biggest show of the year, and His Worship the Lord Mayor is coming to open it.'

'Always business with you, Fitz,' spat Dru's father. 'You talk of big shows, of pulling the crowds. But what about my son?'

'Pierre, good publicity is just what we need – and just what Dru needs! The more money we raise, the better defence we can pay for in court. If we can get the crowd on our side, or better still impress the Lord Mayor, then we have a real chance of swinging the trial our way. The mayor might even intervene. He could get Dru released on lack of evidence!'

The mayor's a good man, Lizzie thought. *He gave me food and money when I was starving and had nowhere to go, didn't he? If anyone can help Dru, he can. Fitzy's right. I have to win him over.*

'Any questions?' Fitz waited a moment, then clapped briskly. 'Very well. Back to work, everyone. Let's get ready for the show of a lifetime.'

Once the last of the circus folk had left the tent, only the Penny Gaff Gang were left. Lizzie urged them to get on with their practice, but none of them listened.

'This isn't just on you,' Malachy assured Lizzie.

'We all said we were in this together, remember?'

'We did,' said Erin, nodding.

'All for one and one for all,' added Nora.

'But Malachy, your dad said the best help we can give Dru is to put on a good show!' Lizzie paced back and forth, twisting her fingers together. 'What else can we do for him now?'

'We need to track down the real Phantom,' Malachy said.

'That's what got us into this mess!'

'And the only way out is to keep going. Dad's right about the show being important, but he knows that's just a gamble. We can't change the public's mind about us just from one show, and we can't rely on the Lord Mayor to plead Dru's case for us.'

'He is a toff, after all,' Erin said with a sniff.

'So we deal with this our way.' Malachy pulled a folded newspaper out of his back pocket and pointed to the headline:

PHANTOM TRIAL SET FOR TUESDAY 13TH

'We have to do it fast. Dru goes to trial in three days,' he said sombrely.

Nora stared. 'That soon?'

'If the worst comes to the worst,' Lizzie said, swallowing hard, 'and they do find him guilty, then he'll swing, won't he?'

'Yes,' Hari said simply, before anyone else could answer. 'Robbery is a capital crime. He'll hang for it.'

Lizzie felt a sudden pang of guilt. In her caravan, not so long ago, Dru had pleaded with her to read his palm, but she'd refused.

But what if she had? Could she have seen the arrest, the imprisonment? Could she have warned him? He would have listened, she knew that for certain. Dru trusted her. She imagined taking his warm open hand in hers, exploring the creases on his palm. If she could see his life line now, would it be long … or tragically short?

Angry tears pricked her eyes again, but she blinked them back.

She didn't let herself cry until later, when she was alone in her caravan.

'It's not fair!' she whispered to herself, wiping

streaming tears away. 'Malachy reckons my gift's meant to help people, but all I've done so far is stop toffs from being robbed! What kind of a gift is that? Who cares about rich toffs, anyway?'

She heaved a sob and kicked the wall of the caravan in anger. Then she did it again, wishing she could kick down the walls of Dru's prison cell. She grabbed a flowerpot and smashed it viciously against the wall. That only reminded her of the tile she'd knocked off the roof. It was too much.

Her voice rose in a howl of rage and despair. 'What's the point of having these special powers if I can't help the people I care about?'

CHAPTER 14

The children at the bathing lake in Victoria Park screamed in delight. 'Mummy! Mummy, come and see the ELEPHANTS!'

Lizzie and Hari led Akula and Sashi down into the water, whispering reassuring words of calm while the crowds of children came running up and adults yelled to one another to come and see. Now that the circus had set up here, it was time to get the word out – and nothing attracted attention quite like the elephants.

Akula waded in and dipped her trunk into the water. Some of the more daring boys and girls edged closer, and one even reached out to touch her flank.

'Remember to come and see her this evening!' Lizzie announced. 'She'll be performing for the Lord Mayor himself. Only a few tickets left!'

On cue, Sashi blew a glittering spray of water into the air, spattering the squealing children.

It was late afternoon when they led Akula and Sashi back to their enclosure. Excitement was building for the Lord Mayor's arrival. By the look of it, Dru's arrest hadn't hurt business one bit – there were crowds at all the sideshows and the evening show was sold out. A few touts who'd had the foresight to buy up tickets were selling them on at an outrageous price, though not where Fitzy could see them.

That evening, the Lord Mayor finally made his grand entrance. The crush at the park gates was too thick for any of the Penny Gaff Gang to see what was going on. Lizzie ended up perched on Akula's back, shading her eyes to see over the crowd, telling the others what was happening.

'There he is! I see him! He's got a red robe on, with a big gold chain!'

'Is my dad there?' Malachy asked eagerly.

'Yes, I can see his topper. The mayor's shaking his hand. Like they're old pals.'

There was a burst of applause from the onlookers. Everybody heard it.

'Who else is there?' Erin asked. 'Did Princess Alexandra come?'

'Can't see her.'

'See, Nora, I told you she wouldn't!'

'There's a right crowd of toffs with the mayor, though. Men in tailcoats with huge beards, mostly. Some bloke in a military coat with loads of medals. And an old woman all done up like a peacock.' She looked again. 'They're on the move. They're coming!'

'Get to your places, everyone!' Malachy yelled. 'Looks like the mayor wants a tour of the circus. Dad said he might. Give it your best, because Dru's counting on us.'

Lizzie sprinted to the fortune-teller's tent and quickly pulled her robes and veil on. Her heart was thumping as she waited to hear the mayor's voice outside the tent and it seemed only minutes later when she heard the sound of an approaching crowd, and Fitzy's voice ringing out over it. 'Now, why don't we begin with a visit to the only genuine clairvoyant to be found in any circus in the land – the Magnificent Lizzie Brown!'

'I happen to be a spiritualist, and I will have you

know there are a great many genuine clairvoyants!' she heard a posh woman say, sounding offended.

'Ah, but madam, they are not to be found in circuses,' Fitzy said with smooth good humour. The gentlemen guffawed at that.

Oh Gawd, I'm the first act he's going to see, Lizzie thought, feeling a little faint. *Please don't let me mess this up.* One of the smaller crystal balls looked dirty. She picked it up and gave it a quick polish.

'I've heard amazing things about this woman,' the mayor said. 'How on earth did you ever come across her?'

'Fate,' said Fitzy. Lizzie knew his eyes would be twinkling. 'Your Worship, would you care to experience her talents for yourself?'

'Well, I don't see why not.'

Lizzie heard the sound of tramping feet, very, very close now. She quickly tucked the grubby little crystal ball into her pocket.

'One moment!' said the mayor from right outside. 'Ladies, gentlemen, you had better leave me alone for this. After all, if this Magnificent Miss Brown is as good as Fitzgerald claims, she may ferret out some of my secrets! And some of you schemers already have your eye on the mayor's seat, eh, Brundell? Eh, Harpole? You'd love to dig up a bit of dirt on me, wouldn't you? Ha-ha! Go on! Be off with you!'

With a great deal of good-natured laughter, the crowd moved on.

Lizzie watched the tent flap move aside, and next thing she knew, the mayor himself was in the tent with her.

'Good heavens,' he said, sitting down. 'Hello, young lady. I expected someone as ancient as myself.'

Lizzie couldn't speak. This task was too important. The words bottlenecked in her throat and wouldn't come out.

'It's the left hand you need, isn't it?' The mayor pulled off his glove a finger at a time and held his hand out, palm up.

'You don't remember me, do you?' Lizzie managed to say. She hadn't meant to say that at all.

The mayor peered at her. 'Lift your veil.'

So Lizzie did.

His eyes widened a little, and he smiled. 'So, we meet again. Isn't fate a peculiar thing?'

'You were kind to me,' she said. 'You gave me money and food, and I didn't even say thank you. So I want to … thank you. I wouldn't be here if it weren't for you, and that's the truth.'

'Lizzie,' said the mayor, 'it was my pleasure to help. We're not so dissimilar, you and I. I think I mentioned that.'

'You did.'

'But I didn't tell you everything. My mother died when I was very young. My father lost his job at the glassworks, because the manager wanted the job for his own son.' He paused and looked disgusted with himself. 'I'm sorry. I must seem like a self-pitying fool. A ridiculous old man, pouring out the story of my life.'

Lizzie tried not to smile. '*I* ought to be telling you your life story! It's meant to be my job.'

'I'll make sure to leave a few bits out,' the mayor smiled. 'You can work for your tuppence! Hard work's how I got to where I am today. I started with nothing.'

'I can't charge you, sir. Wouldn't dream of it.' Lizzie took his palm in hers. She felt for the first time how gnarled and callused the Lord Mayor's hands were. Not like a gentleman's hands at all. *What an amazing man we have running this city*, she thought. He'd come from the gutter, just like her. But he'd pulled himself up and out.

She found the life line and gently began to trace it. Blurry images arose in her mind. The mayor as a young man, working in a slaughterhouse, retching at the smell. Lizzie caught a whiff of it and her stomach heaved. A plump overseer in a top hat cuffed his ear, and shouted at him to get back to work. Then he was carrying heavy luggage along a dock. A wealthy man in a fine coat sneered at him as he carried the cases up a ship's gangplank. "Put it down here, you guttersnipe," barked the rich man. *The mayor's had a hard life,* Lizzie thought.

Without warning a flash of pain exploded behind her eyes. She gasped at the suddenness of it, like biting into ice when you have a sore tooth, and almost let go of the mayor's hand, but she knew she had to hold on. Whatever she was about to see was important.

The pain ebbed a little and bright images began to dance across her inner vision, as clear as if she were standing there. She was seeing the evening show. *The future, less than an hour away!*

Erin and Nora went cantering past, standing up in the saddle, broad smiles on their faces. Rice Pudding Pete smacked another clown around the face with a fish. Collette stepped out onto the high wire.

Was Dru there? Had he been released? She strained to see...

Her vision's 'eye' soared up, past the shocked-looking faces of the audience, and down past them into the shadows beyond the stalls. Gooseflesh spread over Lizzie's arms as she saw a familiar hunched-over shape edging forward into the light.

It seemed to give off evil like a powerful stink. Like the taste of blood in your mouth.

Lizzie knew what she would see when it lifted its head. And she could no more look away than a person trapped in a nightmare can force himself to wake up.

The Phantom looked straight at her. The skull-like mask shone a hideous green under the limelight. She felt herself drawn into the dark pits of his black eyes, dragged down to be devoured alive.

'Phantom,' she said in a hollow voice. All she could think was: *I have to warn the mayor!*

The mayor jerked his hand out of her grip. All the colour drained from his face. 'Phantom? What do you mean, girl?'

Lizzie shook her head, trying to come back to her senses. 'I ... I seen him! I think he's after you next!'

'But the Phantom was caught. He's in prison.'

All the friendliness had gone from the mayor's face now. He was looking at her as if she was … a freak.

'I seen him before,' she pleaded. 'There was this bloke, he came for a reading, and I saw the Phantom coming to rob his house. But the bloke didn't listen, so we stopped the robbery ourselves. You've got to believe me!'

He looked at her curiously. 'So. The Phantom is still at large, and coming after the Lord Mayor of London? This has to be the strangest fortune ever told.'

He'll have me locked in the bedlam-house for this, Lizzie thought. *With all the other freaks and loonies.*

'The Phantom knows you're here tonight, don't he?' she said desperately. 'It's been in all the papers. He's dangerous. And now he knows where to find you!'

For one sweet moment, she actually thought he might take her seriously.

Then he laughed. 'Look here, Miss Lizzie Brown. I'm glad I helped you, and you're a plucky little thing. But I'm afraid you've fallen for your own act – hook, line and sinker! I wish you the best of luck but you must remember it's only a circus act. Would you do that, for me?'

He stood up and threw the tent curtain open,

stopped just outside and turned around. 'And if you do want to earn a living, I'd stop talking about Phantoms and bugaboos if I were you. Tall dark strangers and long journeys by sea, that's what people want.'

Fitzy was waiting outside. 'How was she, Your Worship?'

'Most entertaining!' laughed the mayor. 'So, what about this lion of yours, then?'

Lizzie sat there in the dark, shaken. No, she couldn't bear this alone. She had to find Malachy. She hung the *BACK IN FIVE MINUTES* sign outside her tent and ran, still in her mystic robes.

He came straight to the door of his trailer when he heard her hammering on it. 'Blimey, Lizzie. Are you all right?'

'No,' she said, feeling her face start to crumple. 'No, I'm ruddy not all right!'

'Sit down.'

He fetched her a glass of water. While she sipped it gratefully, shivering in the seat, he found a warm shawl and wrapped it around her shoulders. Once he'd done all he could to make her comfortable, he asked her gently what was wrong.

'I was doing the mayor's reading, and I saw the

Phantom again,' she said. Some of the water went down the wrong way and she choked and coughed. Malachy waited patiently until she could speak again. 'I think he's going to attack the mayor tonight.'

'What exactly did you see?'

'Just the circus, the acts going out, and the Phantom in the shadows. He was angry, so angry! I could feel it, Mal. He was going to kill someone.' She rubbed her aching forehead. 'We have to stop him this time. I won't let him hurt the mayor. He's a good man. People don't know how good he is.'

'But why would the Phantom want to kill him?' Malachy wondered. 'Everyone in the city loves him. Unless… Of course! That's it!'

'What?'

'We're all hoping to get the mayor to help out with Dru's trial, remember? But the Phantom must want Dru to be found guilty. Dru will be hanged in place of him!'

'So the Phantom must have guessed we'd be counting on the mayor's support to get Dru off.'

Malachy looked grim. 'Exactly. And with the rest of the gang in the show, there's only you and me that can stop him.'

'We could talk to your dad, get him to cancel the show—'

'There's no time for that! It's starting in a few minutes. Tell me more about what you saw, Lizzie. Anything that could help.'

Lizzie shrugged. 'There's no more to tell. I just saw the Phantom standing there past the crowd, in the dark, near the edge of the tent.'

'And the show was in progress,' Malachy mused. 'So either he's planning to sneak in once the show's started…'

'…or he's here already,' Lizzie finished. 'Inside the tent. Just waitin' for the right moment to strike. I have to get to the mayor!'

CHAPTER 15

As Lizzie headed out of Fitzy's caravan with Malachy close behind, she heard a smash and a scream.

Anita came running out of her own caravan, pale and shocked. 'Someone's chucking stones! My window's broke!'

More stones thumped against the roofs and walls of the trailers. Shouts rang out: 'Freaks!', 'Thieves!', 'Pack up and go somewhere else!'

The Amazon Queen came running from the edge of the site. 'There's a mob,' she panted. 'Throwin' stones at the caravans.'

Lizzie badly needed to run and find the mayor. But

Anita's face was full of fear and Lizzie knew she couldn't leave the tiny lady on her own. 'Mally, you'd better go and tell Fitzy,' she said. 'I'll stay here.'

The Amazon Queen pointed. 'He's on his way already, look. He's brought half the acts with him!'

Lizzie felt bolder now that Fitzy was storming across the ground towards her. The mayor wasn't with him. Of course not – this wasn't part of the official tour.

She peered around the caravans to get a look at the mob. There were about fifty of them. Instead of going to the gates at the front, they'd crossed the park to the rear of the circus where the trailers were. They stood in a mass like a pack of hungry wolves waiting to spring, hurling stones and jeers, but always staying just on the far side of the staked-out perimeter of the circus camp.

'Take this, you thieving scum!' a man yelled as he ran forward. He pitched a huge stone as hard as he could. Lizzie stood paralysed, staring into the crowd, as it arced through the air and flew straight towards her face.

Malachy tugged her out of its path at the last moment and the stone whacked into the dirt. 'Lizzie, wake up! What's the matter?'

'He's here,' she stammered. 'When that bloke ran

out, I saw him.'

'Saw who?' Malachy leaned in and said in a whisper, 'The Phantom?'

Lizzie shook her head. 'No.' She pointed. 'My pa.'

It was definitely him in the midst of them, bellowing like an ape, picking up stones and lobbing them along with the rest. Lizzie hid her face. If he noticed her now, he'd take her back for sure, especially with the mob on his side.

Thank God, she thought, as Fitzy came striding out to meet the angry crowd. His face bore a showman's grin, but there was a dangerous look in his eyes, and Bungo and Joey walked close behind him, carrying mallets that they swung menacingly.

Fitzy held up his hands, and that alone seemed to quieten the crowd a little. *Nobody could resist the man's charm*, Lizzie thought. But for how long?

'I'm afraid the tickets are sold out! We're about to start. Please go home!'

'*We're* not here for your show!' someone shouted.

'I see. What seems to be the problem?'

The boldest stone-thrower brandished a newspaper at him. 'Your boy Dru Boisset, mate! He's the problem! Robbin' the good folk of London!'

'We've all read about him!' someone yelled.

'You're a pack of thievin' lowlifes!' screamed a woman. By the sound of her, she was drunk. 'We're goin' to come on there and take back all them things he stole! Just you try an' stop us!'

The mob began to edge forward again, shouting angrily. Lizzie knew they wouldn't find any stolen goods in the caravans. But that wouldn't stop them from helping themselves to whatever they liked.

'Looks like there's going to be a dust-up,' Fitzy sighed. He took off his top hat and passed it to Malachy. 'Keep that safe for me, lad. I'm due to open the show in ten minutes, and I don't want to look like a scruff.'

Lizzie could clearly see her father now through the crowd. He was rolling up his sleeves, baring his huge arms. She knew all too well what that meant. *As if knocking me about weren't enough. Now he's going to hit my friends too.*

Then a fresh stab of cold fear went through her as she caught a glimpse of who was standing behind him. Tousled hair, pale face – was that Madame Aurora?

'Get 'em!' someone screamed from the back of the mob.

The crowd surged forward and broke through the

perimeter, yelling and screaming. Fitzy and the others met their charge head-on and from that moment on, it was every man for himself. Circus folk fought with rioters, rolling and tumbling in the dust. Lizzie saw one of the clowns stagger back from the brawl with blood pouring from his nose. Next moment, the Amazon Queen knocked his attacker cold with a single punch.

'Come on,' Malachy told Lizzie, tugging her arm. 'You'd better get out of here.'

'Fitzy, where's the mayor?' she demanded.

'Having a slice of cake in Ma Sullivan's tea tent!' Fitzy shouted. 'Tell him I won't be long!'

Lizzie ran, with a quick glance over her shoulder. She saw Mario lift his colossal arms and bellow like a bull, then charge right into the thick of the fighting. He flung rioters this way and that, picking them up off the ground and hurling them off the circus site. A few of the attackers ran away, too terrified of Mario to continue. Then Lizzie was away, the yells ringing in her ears.

Thoughts raced through Lizzie's head as she headed for the tea tent, which was on the far side of the site, away from caravans and the show tent alike. If her vision hadn't been wrong, tonight she would meet the Phantom face to face.

Could it be her father? The voice she'd heard hadn't sounded like his, but he could have been putting another voice on. He was used to disguising himself when he went out begging. And she'd just seen him moments before, chucking stones with the rest of the mob.

If it wasn't him, then who?

She thought back to the reading she'd done for the round-faced man, who had been so sceptical. It was a good job the Phantom hadn't hurt him as she had feared, though somehow he'd taken the keys off him without a fight.

Lizzie frowned. Now she thought about it, she hadn't heard anything about the Phantom robbing a bunch of keys from the caretaker. Surely, if the Phantom had taken the man's keys, he'd have told the police?

A nagging voice at the back of her mind was whispering a question: *Out of all those keys, how did the Phantom know exactly which one to use to let himself in the back door?* Lizzie gasped out loud. 'No,' she said to herself. 'I don't believe it. It can't have been him!'

What had Hari said? The Phantom wears a mask because he's ashamed. *Ashamed of robbing the property he was meant to be safeguarding, perhaps?*

The Lord Mayor had to know! She put on a fresh burst of speed. *I'll catch you*, she thought. *You think you're so clever, but I know who you are. I'll have the last laugh, just you see!*

She threw open the flap of the tea tent. There was nobody inside at all. The long tables were abandoned. Even the trestle table where Ma Sullivan made the tea was empty.

'Hello?' she called. 'Your Worship? Are you there?'

Nobody answered her. Lizzie began to feel uneasy. Had the mayor left for the show already? She looked around the tea tent for some kind of clue, but there was nothing. Not even crumbs.

'He must have gone in,' she muttered to herself. She looked out across the site and saw the circus folk making their way to the show tent, ready to start. There was Fitzy, top hat back on his head again. They must have beaten back the mob.

She left the tea tent and headed off across the grass. *Going to have to push through the crowds and reach the Lord Mayor in the audience*, she thought. But just then, she heard something behind her.

Footsteps, hard and fast, like someone running.

She spun around. A dark shape dodged back into the shadows, vanishing behind two storage tents. Lizzie swallowed. Of all the people who might wish to do her harm, she could only think of one who knew their way around a circus campsite well enough to tail her through it, and that was the woman who had been the fortune-teller before her.

Better run the rest of the way!

She lifted her mystic robes and ran. The show tent loomed up ahead of her. Crowds were bustling at the main entrance, and a hubbub of excited conversation reached her ears. Her heart lurched. *They're letting them in already! Don't tell me I'm too late!* But the sight of the big crowds gave her courage. If she could reach them, she could dive into them and her pursuer couldn't follow.

Those running feet were pounding behind her again. Closer, this time. She knew who was coming. Madame Aurora had sworn to take revenge on her. Now she was going to fulfil that promise. Lizzie put on a burst of speed. She heard her pursuer do the same. It sounded like Aurora was right behind her!

She looked over her shoulder – and let out a terrified cry.

It wasn't Madame Aurora bearing down on her at all. It was the figure she'd seen in her nightmares. A man in a mask like a screaming skull – not the battered old mask she'd seen before, but brand new and gleaming white.

The mask of the Phantom!

CHAPTER 16

There was only one thing for it. Run!

Lizzie ran for the safety of the show tent, towards the lights and the crowds of people. Her chest hurt and she gasped for breath as she put on even more speed.

Behind her, she heard the Phantom grunting and panting as he tried to catch up. Ahead, someone was coming out of the crowd, moving towards her. The light behind him cast a long three-legged shadow across the grass. She prayed it was a friend.

Wait – three-legged shadow?

It was Malachy, hobbling towards her on his crutch. He saw who was following, waved frantically and yelled out a warning: 'It's him! The Phantom's here!'

'I know!' Lizzie shrieked. 'Get to the mayor!'

Malachy ignored her. He kept coming in her direction, swinging as fast as he could on his crutch and one good leg.

Lizzie glanced over her shoulder. The Phantom was almost upon her now, but he was staggering and winded. If she was lucky, Malachy might reach her before he did. Not that two would have much more of a chance than one against him...

Malachy and the Phantom reached Lizzie at the exact same moment. Malachy blocked the Phantom's path, while Lizzie ducked around him.

'Run!' he shouted. 'I'll slow him down!'

'You won't,' the Phantom snorted in his hoarse put-on voice. Without breaking stride, he thrust out an arm into Malachy's chest. The boy fell backwards and went sprawling on the grass. The Phantom laughed, a gross-sounding chuckle.

My goose is cooked, Lizzie thought. The safety of the show tent was still a hundred paces away. It might as well have been a hundred miles.

But as the Phantom lunged to grab her by the hair, Malachy let out a yell and flung his crutch. It spun through the air and caught the Phantom below the knees. The Phantom stumbled and fell.

'Keep running!' Malachy shouted. 'Get to the show tent. There's too many people in there for him to do anything.'

Lizzie ran for her life. She was sick with fear of what the Phantom might do to Malachy, but she couldn't turn around again, not now.

As the Phantom struggled to his feet, he staggered for a moment like a drunken man, then came after her with fresh strength. But now he was limping from where Malachy's crutch had caught his legs. Grunts of pain came from him every time he moved.

The lights and noise of the show tent loomed closer. *Almost there now*, Lizzie told herself. *Come on, girl. You can do it!*

But even as she ran, she realized she couldn't go in through the front after all. There were just too many people to push through. She'd never reach the mayor in time.

She changed direction and ran towards the back of the tent, into the dark shadows where the animal cages were. She dived down at the ground.

Next moment she was pulling up the edge of the

tent, wriggling under the damp canvas fabric, and crawling in. She could smell the moist grass, the sweat from the horses, the soft warm smell of the whale-oil lanterns. Smells that meant safety.

She'd come out behind the rows of raised seating, in a dark cluttered space where the unused scenery was kept. The audience were almost all inside, and the show had already begun.

'Ladies and gentlemen,' said Fitzy's voice, 'I welcome you one and all to a night of dazzling entertainment!' Trumpets blared and cymbals clashed. The crowd roared and applauded heartily.

The wall of the tent bulged beside Lizzie. The canvas flap lifted. The Phantom was fighting his way into the tent. There was only one thing she could do now. She screamed. She took as big a breath as she could and she screamed at the top of her voice.

It wasn't enough. The music and the crowd's roaring drowned the sound of her screams out completely. She felt the ground vibrate under her feet. Hoof beats – Nora and Erin must be riding into the ring to start the show.

Lizzie backed further into the shadows, biting her knuckles in pure terror, while the Phantom struggled under the lip of the tent and pulled himself to his feet. He glanced around, looking for Lizzie, and quickly found her.

He advanced on her, forcing her back up against the tent wall. There was nowhere left to run. As if on cue, the crowd gasped, 'Oooh!'

'Don't fight, girl,' the Phantom rasped, fighting for breath. 'It'll be over a lot quicker if you don't … fight.'

There were so many people in this tent. Any one of them could have saved her from him. But not a single one could hear her. *I'm going to die*, Lizzie realized. *Here in the dark, in this overwhelming din. Nobody's going to find my body until the circus packs up to go.*

The Phantom lunged at her throat with both hands.

Lizzie glimpsed a rope ladder dangling to one side and decided she wasn't ready to die just yet. She leaped up and caught a rung, pulling herself up out of the Phantom's grasp and climbing for all she was worth.

The ladder led up the side of the tent. Lizzie remembered seeing one of the roustabouts climb up it once. She looked up and remembered what it was for. It led all the way up to the highest part of the tent, to where one of the lighting ropes was tethered. Those criss-cross ropes, above even the high wire, held a line of dangling lanterns that lit the circus from the top down. Every night, someone had to clamber up here to light them. She felt the rope ladder shake and glanced down. The Phantom was following her up – and the bang Malachy had given him with his crutch didn't seem to be slowing him down.

Lizzie kept climbing, hand over hand, until she could see the crowds seated below her. The equestrian show was in full swing, with Nora lashing out with her bullwhip, smacking juggling clubs out of the air as Erin threw them.

Look at me! Lizzie wanted to scream. *I'm here!* But the crowd were howling and stamping in their excitement and the band was playing up a storm. Nobody would hear, even if she fell to her death. 'Keep going!' she told herself. 'You can do this!'

On and on she climbed. She was perilously high now, almost at the lighting rope. The Phantom was right below her, grunting as he grabbed rung after rung.

Then, suddenly, she was at the top – and there was nowhere left to go. Despair overwhelmed her. As she looked down at the tiny figures below, the Phantom grabbed her foot! Lizzie gripped the rungs tight and kicked wildly, trying to fling him off the ladder. He was too strong. Now he was pulling her, dragging her down towards him.

Lizzie felt something heavy in her pocket. All at once she remembered the little crystal ball she'd tucked in there. She flung it as hard as she could, straight for the band, hoping she didn't hurt anyone.

CRASH! went a cymbal, completely out of time. The music faltered.

'STOP!' *Fitzy?* Lizzie hardly dared to hope.

The music fell silent. A chorus of gasps went up from the crowd and a light flashed across Lizzie's eyes. Someone was shining a bull's-eye lantern up into the high shadows, trying to find them.

'Up there!' Fitz shouted. 'Up by the third rope!'

The crowd started murmuring in puzzlement. Was this part of the show? Lizzie had only seconds to act. She filled her lungs and let out an ear-splitting scream.

The light found them. Now there were screams from the audience too. Cries of 'Phantom!' rang out all around the ring and Lizzie saw the circus performers staring up at her, pointing in horror. The Phantom hung frozen in place, the lantern light revealing him clearly.

Lizzie would never get this chance again. She took it.

'Let's see who you really are!' With one deft move, she reached down. The Phantom flung up a hand to stop her, but he was a second too late.

Lizzie tore the mask off his face.

CHAPTER 17

Lizzie clung to the rope ladder, dizzyingly high up, and looked down into the snarling face of … the Lord Mayor of London!

'You little fool,' he growled. 'Do you have any idea what you've done? They've seen my face. They've all seen my face!'

'I-I thought you were…' Lizzie couldn't understand what she was seeing. This was all wrong. The Phantom couldn't be the kindly Lord Mayor. Could he?

She couldn't speak. The Lord Mayor was grabbing her by the throat, one large hand pressed against her, squeezing, squeezing…

'Can't let any of them live. They've all seen too much. I'm going to burn this whole place to the ground.'

Screams and shouts rang out from down below. Lizzie could hear Fitzy yelling for people to stay calm, because the situation was under control, but for once his ringmaster's authority wasn't working. A couple of terrified spectators dashed right across the open circus ring and made for the exit. One gentleman drew a revolver from his coat pocket and took careful aim.

The Lord Mayor's fingers felt rock-hard, like a marble statue, where they clamped round her neck. Lizzie tried to prise them off, but she couldn't do it with only one hand, and if she let go with the other, she'd fall.

He lowered himself down by one rung, still keeping his tight grip on her neck. She had to follow. That was when she realized he was holding her body between himself and the man with the revolver.

'That's right,' he hissed. 'Keep moving. Nobody will dare take a shot at me if I've got you as a shield.'

He needs me alive, Lizzie thought. *I'm going to make it through this.*

Then the mayor leaned close and whispered, 'And when I've got out of here, I'm going to kill you. Break your neck like a rabbit, I will.' He giggled, a strange high-pitched sound, the laugh of a man whose mind had broken into pieces. 'They'll fish you out of the Thames in a month, all bloated and green.'

They stepped down another rung.

Lizzie knew he meant it. She was more terrified than she'd ever been in her life. His grip slackened for an instant, long enough for her to jerk her head back and loose his grasp on her neck. Words burst out of her. 'Why are you doing this?'

The Lord Mayor only grunted, like a drunken man woken from sleep.

'It don't make sense!' Lizzie yelled. 'You were so kind to me.' *It's like there's a crack right through his mind*, she thought hastily. *If I can keep pounding away at it, he might break.* 'You gave me food and money,' she said. 'And then you nearly killed that bloke in Spitalfields. Why?'

'He got in my way!' the mayor bellowed. His face was bright red now; Lizzie couldn't tell whether it was from the chase or anger. 'People shouldn't get in my way. I've been waiting years to get my revenge – and I won't let anyone stop me.' He spat the words out in total contempt.

Lizzie guessed her only chance to survive was to

keep him talking. 'Revenge on who?' she asked. 'Tell me what you mean—'

'London's a pit! A pit of dung!' He was really raving now. Little white dots flecked his face. 'You know who the only moral ones are? It's not the police, oh no. It's not the rich toffs who hold their leash. They'd step over the likes of me in the street. Maggots. Threw me out. My father too! No, it's the poor. The starving. The ones who've got nothing.'

Carefully, he lifted his hand and closed it across her throat again. 'This is all *your* fault. If you'd shut your mouth like I told you to, you wouldn't have forced me to do this. Just like that stupid man in Spitalfields I had to batter half to death. He interrupted me. It was his fault.'

Were those tears in his eyes? Lizzie saw his pupils shrink to tiny dots of sheer madness. She remembered what she'd seen when she'd read his palm. His bitterness over the cruelty he'd suffered as a young man had driven him mad. She looked away, knowing what could happen if you looked an unstable person in the eye. She'd learned that from Pa, the hard way.

His fingers dug painfully into her flesh. She wanted to beg him not to hurt her any more, but she knew words wouldn't do any good. She had to let him think he'd won, that she'd given up the fight, so she let her body go limp. He took her weight and climbed down another rung.

Through half-open eyes she watched for something, anything, that could help her to escape. Down at the bottom of the ladder a small crowd had gathered. She recognized Bungo, Joey and Mario, and Fitzy himself. They were looking up at her with grim faces.

'Move aside!' the mayor yelled down to them. 'She's dead if you don't. Want me to throw her down? Think you can catch her, do you?'

Then, out of the corner of her eye, Lizzie saw a shimmering white shape. It was all she could do not to stiffen in excitement and give the game away. It was Collette, racing across to the trapeze with Nora and Erin close behind her.

Quickly they scrambled up to the trapeze. Collette took up position on the bar, hanging from it by her knees. She swung out across the show tent, then swung back and grabbed Nora by the ankles. On the next swing, Nora grabbed Erin by her ankles.

The human chain of three girls swayed back and forth, back and forth, until Nora's outstretched arms could almost reach Lizzie. The mayor hadn't noticed – he was too busy shouting threats at Fitzy and his men. But no matter how close Erin swung, she wasn't close enough to grab. There was only one thing for it – Lizzie would have to pull out of the mayor's grasp and jump.

But it was so far to fall! Lizzie glanced down into the terrifying space below, at all the upturned horrified faces. There was only one safe place for her to land – the safety net in the middle of the show tent. If she timed it right and Erin caught her, they could swing back over it and let her go.

If…

It was a chance.

I can't do it.

The only chance she had.

Erin's pleading face swung back into view. Her arms reached for Lizzie.

But Lizzie froze, like a terrified animal. She couldn't move. The mayor was slowly choking the life out of her and she was just too afraid to fight him.

He's just like Pa, she thought. *Too strong. You can't win against his kind. They always break you in the end.*

'Come on, Lizzie!' Nora shouted. 'You can do this!'

The mayor seemed to snap out of a trance. He

suddenly noticed the three girls swinging towards him. A roar of encouragement came from the crowd, cheering Lizzie on.

'No,' he gasped. 'Got to finish you off. Now.' His grip tightened around her neck, crushing her windpipe.

Lizzie twisted her head around and bit the mayor. Her teeth sank into his sweaty arm. She bit deep and hard like a terrier and kept biting down until her jaw ached and hot coppery blood filled her mouth. The mayor gave a shrill scream and let go of her throat.

Time now seemed to slow down. Lizzie could see Erin swinging up and towards her and she turned and flung herself off the rope ladder – out into empty space.

The crowd gasped as one.

Lizzie fell, her arms stretched out and grasping at nothing. She felt weightless as an angel. The circus lights rocketed past like shooting stars around her.

Next second, Erin's hands clasped hers.

No longer falling but swinging, she hurtled down past the hundreds of astonished faces, down and down, faster and faster. Too late, she realized her hands were slick with sweat and she was losing her grip.

The net was up ahead, but Lizzie wasn't going to reach it. One of her hands broke free. She knew she was going to hit the sawdust-strewn gap and miss the net completely.

Erin tried to snatch her flailing hand back. Their fingers brushed, but Lizzie couldn't reach.

With all the strength left in her body, Lizzie held on with her remaining hand. Her arm was agony, almost ripped out of its socket, but she held on until finally her fingers could no longer grip ... and she let go.

Instead of the back-breaking impact she'd expected, she hit something taut and strong that flung her back up again, then caught her and held her in its safe embrace.

The net. I made it to the net!

The very edge of the net, she saw as she sat up, dazed. She'd been two feet away from certain death.

Erin, Nora and Collette gracefully tumbled down, making the whole net bounce like a trampoline.

Lizzie looked around, astonished to be still alive, as Fitzy and his men went rushing up the rope ladder. With his hostage gone, all the mayor could do was cling there at the top and wait to be dragged down. There was nothing terrifying about him now. He looked miserable and pathetic, a broken old man.

Bungo flung him over his back and came back down

the ladder. He carried the mayor in front of the crowd like a trophy.

'Here is your Phantom, ladies and gentlemen!' Fitzy shouted triumphantly. 'The real villain, unmasked before your very eyes. Take a good look while you can, because he'll be going away for a long, long time.'

CHAPTER 18

'Flippin' heck!'

Lizzie couldn't remember ever seeing a finer breakfast than the one Erin and Nora brought in to her: bacon, mushrooms, tomatoes, toast, and some sort of flaky thing like a crescent moon that smelled delicious.

'It's a croissant,' explained Nora. 'French nosh. She thought you might like to try one.'

'Madame Boisset must have took hours to do this!' Lizzie bit into it eagerly. It was like tasting the summer sun.

'Actually, Collette made all this for you,' Erin said.

Lizzie brushed crumbs from her dress. 'I have to

go and say thanks.'

'You'll have to do it later. They've all gone off to fetch Dru from the prison.'

Lizzie's eyes widened. 'You mean…'

'He got a full pardon!' Nora squealed. 'They're letting him go.'

As they hugged, Malachy and Hari knocked on the door, waving a newspaper and chanting the headlines to the whole campsite:

'Read all about it!'

'Phantom unmasked!'

'Lord Mayor of London arrested and shamed!'

'Get in here with that paper, you pair of eejits,' Erin said. 'We all want to hear what they've got to say.'

'For once,' Nora grinned.

They sat together while Malachy read the front-page news aloud to them. Lizzie could hardly believe what she was hearing. With the Lord Mayor in custody, the full story was finally coming out and she could understand the meaning of the strange words he'd hissed at her the night before.

'"Word of the so-called Phantom scandal has already reached as far as New York and Hong Kong,"' Malachy read in a posh voice, pinching his nose shut so he would sound funnier. "'Lord Mayor Albert Goswin, noted philanthropist and champion of the poor, has been revealed as a hater of the rich. We can now reveal that his habit of robbing the houses of the wealthy stems from his boyhood of desperate poverty. The Phantom's crimes are nothing less than a campaign of revenge against the privileged classes, who the former mayor believes to be responsible for the misery of his youth.'"

Lizzie listened with amazement as Malachy read out the story. The mayor was haunted by the fear that one day he might be poor and hungry again. So he punished the rich, stealing their treasures and hiding them away.

'So that is why none of the stolen goods ever appeared again,' Hari said. 'He wasn't selling them on as most thieves would do. He was hoarding them.'

'But how was he doing it?' Nora asked.

'I'm coming to that,' Malachy said. "'Owing to his position of authority, the former mayor could visit any police station in the city and enjoy unsupervised access to police records. In this way he not only discovered which houses held the most valuable treasures, he was able to steal the duplicate keys that the householders had left with the police to ensure their protection.'"

'So *that's* how he got those keys!' Lizzie said with a laugh, thinking of the round-faced watchman.

'An elegant plan.' Hari sounded like he admired it.

'A barmy plan, more like,' Malachy said. 'He was off his head. The paper thinks so too: "The success of his many robberies over the years convinced the Phantom he had a grand destiny. He fancied himself the true King of London, ruling from his pile of stolen gold, with the people of the city terrified to speak his name. Those who got in his way were swiftly punished, often in the most violent and brutal manner. Rich and poor alike were cut down in his wrath."'

'Don't I know it,' Lizzie said with a shiver. She remembered the Phantom's hands around her neck, squeezing mercilessly, and she touched the purple bruises he'd left there. But even though he'd nearly killed her, a small part of her couldn't help feeling sorry for the mayor. She'd seen herself in Rat's Castle how living in poverty and squalor could drive people insane.

A commotion outside the caravan told them something important had happened. They rushed out to see the circus folk excitedly dashing from their own trailers and heading for a gathering crowd at the gate.

Lizzie caught sight of a familiar figure riding high

on his father's shoulders, and her heart leaped into her mouth.

'Dru! It's Dru! He's back!'

And they all went stampeding over to meet the Boissets.

'Everything they tell you about Newgate? It is true,' Dru said, accepting a cup of coffee from his mother. 'Rats the size of Akula. Stinking filth in all the cells. Lice! Dead bodies carried out every day! I had to share a cell with a man with brown teeth – a murderer, they said. It was a relief when they took him out and hanged him.'

A party had broken out in Ma Sullivan's tea tent. Dru was holding everyone spellbound with stories of his brief time in prison.

'Oh, Lizzie? I ran into someone you know.'

'My pa?'

Dru grinned. 'Madame Aurora. They dragged her in on my second day – I guess she couldn't give up the stealing after all.'

'She'll be out in three months,' Malachy said sourly.

'No she won't. She's been sentenced to transportation! *Bon voyage.*'

Lizzie felt a blessed relief. In London, Madame Aurora was a danger, but in Australia? She'd never threaten Lizzie again.

Fitzy drained his cup of tea. 'Well, folks, I hate to break up the party, but there's work to do. Now that Dru's back, it's time to move on. We set off for Kensal Green tomorrow morning.'

'Fitzy's is back in business!' Malachy said, and flipped one of his father's hats onto his head in a single throw.

One by one, people began to move away. There were a hundred jobs to do, and precious little time for celebrating. Eventually, only Nora and Lizzie were left, sitting on the caravan roof and watching the circus dismantle itself.

'So, how's it feel to be a hero?' Nora asked with a smile.

'You tell me,' Lizzie shrugged. 'If you three hadn't caught me, I'd be brown bread.'

'Oh, c'mon. Be serious. What about that gift of yours? All the things Malachy said? Don't you think you've got a destiny?'

'The Phantom thought he had a destiny,' Lizzie said.

'I don't think I like *destinies*. They mess you up. Drive you mad. My gift, though? That's real enough. I've seen the results.'

'So … you're going to keep at it, then? Solving crimes and helping people and that?'

'Course I am,' Lizzie said seriously. 'Look. I don't understand *how* I can see this stuff. Don't s'pose I ever will. But I reckon I should use it to do good things. That's simpler than all this destiny rubbish.' She knocked back the last of her tea and looked into the empty cup. 'I've never made a difference in the world before. I don't want to stop now. Not ever.'

'Never ever?'

'So long as the visions keep coming, I'll keep using them to try setting things right.'

Nora leaned her head on her friend's shoulder. 'You're a good person. And a good friend.'

'Better than my pa, I hope. Maybe that's why I've got the power. To make up for all the bad things Pa does. Like a balance.'

They sat in silence for a moment.

'Come on,' Nora said. 'Let's go see to the horses. Long trip tomorrow.'

As the girls were walking towards the animal trailers,

a shout made Lizzie stop in her tracks.

'Oi! Lizzie Brown! You stop right there!'

She turned to see her father striding towards her, his sleeves rolled up, his jaw thrust forward. He was stone-cold sober and furious.

'You're not allowed here!' she yelled. 'Leave me alone!'

He grabbed her arm in his iron grip. 'Shut your yap or I'll shut it for you. You're coming home.'

'I won't! You can't make m— Ow!'

He began to drag her off. 'I ruddy can, you little good-for-nothing sow. You've been earning, you have. Behind my back. That money's mine.'

'You're hurting me! Get off!' Lizzie's voice rose to a scream.

Nora took her other arm and pulled, trying to drag Lizzie away from her father. Pa sneered at her, lifted his hand and smacked her around the face. She stumbled back, her hand to her cheek, her eyes watering. 'That's what you get!' Pa said, shaking a fist. 'You want some more?'

'HITTING GIRLS, ARE YOU?' Pierre Boisset came storming over, with Fitzy, Mario and some other circus hands close behind. 'BIG MAN, ARE YOU?'

Pa set his hands on his hips. 'What're you going to do about it, Froggy?'

'Let her go!'

'Make me!'

Pierre shrugged. 'As you wish.' Then, faster than a whip crack, his fist shot out and hit Pa right on his jaw.

Pa staggered like a drunken elephant. Pierre's second punch went into his stomach, doubling him over. He then hooked a foot behind Pa's ankle and shoved, sending the man sprawling on the grass, coughing and spluttering.

Fitzy held Pierre back before he could start kicking Pa in the ribs. 'I think he's had enough.'

Pa levered himself up on his elbows. 'You're the boss 'ere, right?'

'I am.'

'That girl's mine. I'm her father.'

'So I gathered.'

'You've got no right to keep her!' Pa roared. 'She's coming with me!'

Fitzy turned to Lizzie. 'I'm afraid he's right. I have no right to keep you here. If you'd rather go home, just say the word.'

Pale and trembling, Lizzie looked her father right

in the eye. 'No. I don't want to go home, thanks all the same.'

'I know why you want her.' Pa coughed. 'She's worth money. She's famous now. She ought to be earning for me!'

'Her decision is made. You heard. Good day.'

'Now just you wait a minute—'

'*Good day*, sir.'

Fitzy nodded to Mario, who went and lifted Pa up by the scruff of the neck. The last Lizzie saw of her father, he was being carried across the park, kicking his legs in the air.

'Are you sure about this?' Nora asked.

Lizzie hugged her friend. 'More than anything in my life.'

It was the final show in Victoria Park, and the show tent was packed with eager customers. One more special performance, in honour of the Phantom's brave unmasker? Nobody wanted to miss that!

Fitzy had an announcement to make:

'Before we move on tomorrow, it is my pleasure

to introduce one last show. Normally I would ask the audience to show their appreciation for the performers, but tonight, both audience and performers show their appreciation for one young lady!'

Fitzy bowed to Lizzie where she sat. He gestured for her to stand, so Lizzie rose and took a shy bow, while a storm of applause rained down on her.

A whole show, just for me. I never could have dreamed it in all my days.

The next hour passed like a dream. The Sullivans performed their most daring horse tricks, finishing off by balancing into an 'L' shape standing on the backs of their two biggest golden horses, which made Lizzie gasp with excitement.

Dru walked along the highest of the high wires, juggling some skittles as he went. He called out, in the hoarse Cockney tones of a newspaper-seller: 'Read all about it! The Magnificent Lizzie Brown bags herself a Phantom!'

The clowns trooped in, arms over one another's shoulders, belting out a song:

> *Oh, have you heard the story*
> *They tell all round the town,*

Of the girl what caught the Phantom
And pulled his trousers down?
He may have been a menace
But she made him look a clown,
Now he's banged up in the slammer
'Cos of little Lizzie Brown!

After the clowns came the elephants, with Hari riding Akula at the front. They marched in a full circle, then at his command, knelt down.

With a twinkle in his eye, Fitzy beckoned Lizzie to join them.

As the audience gave her a standing ovation, Lizzie stood next to Akula and waved at the crowd. The elephant wrapped her trunk around Lizzie's waist and lifted her onto her back. As Akula stood up, Lizzie looked out over the cheering crowd. All around the ring, the circus folk – performers and crew alike – stood linking arms smiling at her. Lizzie beamed back, warm in their collective embrace, overjoyed to be part of Fitzy's circus.

This was her family now.

Read on for a sneak peek of the next
Lizzie Brown adventure, THE DEVIL'S HOUND...

CHAPTER 1

'Two hundred and seventeen,' said Lizzie Brown, sighing loudly.

The cow she had just counted looked up at her through the pouring rain and chewed thoughtfully. The bright gold paint on the side of Lizzie's circus wagon declared her to be 'THE MAGNIFICENT LIZZIE BROWN, Mystic Wonder Of Our Age!' and 'Unmasker Of The Notorious London Phantom!' Rain hammered it now as if the heavens were trying to wash away all traces of her former glory.

Right now, Lizzie felt about as magnificent as a soggy sock. Circus life was so intense and exciting when the shows were on that you somehow forgot all the travelling you had to do. It was like falling from a brightly coloured trapeze into a tub of cold, grey porridge.

Nora and Erin, the Incredible Sullivan Twins, were taking it in turns to hold the reins. Their red hair stood out brightly next to Lizzie's own chestnut-brown locks. The horses pulling the wagon were a temperamental new pair, who would be performing with the twins, so the girls were doing their own driving for a change. They softly sang Irish folk songs together to the rhythm of the jolting caravan. Lizzie didn't know the tunes, so she'd decided to count cows.

'What in the world are you doing that for?' Erin asked.

'It passes the time,' said Lizzie with a shrug.

And what a lot of time there was to pass. Fitzy's Travelling Circus had been plodding its way through mile after mile of North London countryside for hours now. Lizzie was sick and tired of quaint stone bridges, sullen young men on haycarts and groups outside village pubs staring at the circus as it went past. *Good manners don't cost anything*, her mum had always said.

A shout came from the head of the convoy: 'Kensal Green up ahead!'

Thank goodness, Lizzie thought. *That's our pitch. We can stop soon.*

Although this was the first time the circus had returned to London since Lizzie had joined a month ago, it didn't feel like coming home. Most likely it never would.

London held too many ghosts for Lizzie. Memories of her father's fists, of hunger and begging on the streets, came back to her. Her pa had nearly broken her arms more than once. Sooner or later, in one of his dreadful drunken rages, he'd have broken her neck. That was the way stories like Lizzie's ended in the London slums. Fitzy had saved her from all that, and she'd never forget her debt to him.

The circus had brought her happiness like she'd never known, filling her heart as well as her belly. Compared to the horrors of violence and slow starvation, this endless rain was a small price to pay, especially as she had friends like Nora and Erin to huddle up to. The long journeys might be dull sometimes, but she'd never go back to the life she'd had before.

She'd run away from Rat's Castle, the slum where she'd grown up, only to find a new home among the colourful strangers of Fitzy's Travelling Circus. Fitzy had taken her on as a fortune-teller's assistant, only to discover that he had a *genuine* fortune-teller on his hands.

When her strange powers had first shown themselves, Lizzie had been more surprised than anyone. All that supernatural mystic-shmystic nonsense turning out to be true? It didn't sit right with her, but she couldn't deny it.

All her life she'd had vivid dreams that often came true, but she'd always dismissed it as coincidence. Ironically, it was while the old fortune-teller, Madame Aurora, had been teaching her how to *fake* a reading that her powers had come to the fore. Nowadays, she could see people's futures just by looking into their palms.

Her gift was her living now that she worked at Fitzy's. People paid well for a reading from the Magnificent Lizzie Brown. The sign on her trailer was no idle boast, either. She really had revealed the true identity of the fearsome Phantom, the masked burglar who had terrorized London. It had been the first – and so far only – victory for Lizzie and her crew of crime-fighting circus friends, the Penny Gaff Gang.

'Easy, Victoria!' Nora said, as one of the beautiful black horses pulling their trailer whinnied and tossed her head. 'It's only a cow.'

'What's Kensal Green like, Lizzie?' Erin asked.

'Never been,' Lizzie said. 'Heard there's not much there, though. Railway, canal, a few streets of houses.'

'So long as there's punters to put on a show for, that's what matters,' Nora said.

Lizzie peered ahead, to where dim shapes were coming into view through the misty rainfall. 'Are we at the site yet?'

'We must be!' Erin said.

There was a row of trees just off the road, and as they drew closer Lizzie saw it was the fringe of an enormous park. White stone buildings showed through the trees. The rain brought out the sad, sweet smell of cypresses.

Nora whistled. 'That's a belter of a pitch. Look at all the lawns! Smooth and flat as a billiard table, so they are.'

'Must be a park for proper toffs,' agreed Erin. 'Fitzy knows what he's about. You two beauties will be paid for in no time, won't you now?' She was talking to

Albert and Victoria, the two night-black stunners who were pulling the caravan. Lizzie had never seen more beautiful horses in her life. Fitzy hadn't been able to resist them and had bought them on credit, risking a huge amount of money.

'Come on, Fitzy,' Erin said, frowning. 'Why aren't we heading off the road?'

'Because that ain't our site,' Lizzie said.

'Sure it's not? And how would you know?'

'Because,' Lizzie said with grim satisfaction, 'it ain't the sort of place for a circus to set up. It ain't even a park.'

'So what in the world is it if it's not a park, I'd like to know?'

Before Lizzie could answer, a set of gates came into view. With a silver sound of jingling harnesses and a clop of hooves on stone, a strange procession emerged from the rain and began to pass through the park gates. A gentleman wearing black and carrying an ebony cane walked in front, with a slow measured tread and downcast eyes.

Two gigantic black horses followed, decked out in livery that was as black as their coats. Tall feathery plumes rose from their heads like jets of ink. They were pulling a long, flat carriage that was overflowing with white lilies, startlingly bright against all the black.

In amongst the soaking flowers lay a long, dark casket. Erin and Nora instantly crossed themselves, superstitiously warding off evil in the presence of a dead person. Lizzie might once have smiled at that, but not nowadays.

'It's not a park, it's a cemetery!' Erin exclaimed.

'Kensal Green Cemetery,' said Lizzie, feeling uneasy and proud at the same time. 'Them white buildings are tombs. Goes on for flippin' miles.'

'I've heard about it,' Nora said with a shudder.

'Everybody has,' Erin added. 'The stories they tell … Oh, I hope we're not setting up anywhere near. Me skin's crawling just looking at it.'

The funeral procession went on and on. A host of mourners, women in veils and gentlemen in top hats, passed by with their heads bowed. Many of the women were weeping, swabbing at their eyes with black silk handkerchiefs. The circus people at the front removed their hats respectfully as they passed.

Angry glares were the response. The mourners didn't want to see jolly circus caravans going past. Lizzie heard some of them grumbling: 'Couldn't they have taken a different road?' and, 'How could they? A *circus*? The vulgarity of it!' One woman fainted dramatically and had to be revived with smelling salts. Lizzie felt awkward and shifted uncomfortably.

'There's no call for that,' Nora said. 'Sure it wasn't our fault that we were on the road at the same time as them.'

'Toffs,' Erin snorted, as if that explained everything. 'Think how much that funeral there must have cost! Everything tricked out in black, silks and satins if you please, all for some poor soul who can't even see it!'

Lizzie felt a stab of pain right under her ribs. When her mother had died, there had been no money for a funeral. There hadn't even been a coffin. The man had come and stitched Ma up into the long white sheet. Her father had yelled at her to stop snivelling, but she'd cried anyway. Then her mother had been bundled onto a cart, driven through the streets and lowered with ropes into a hole in the ground. There were other white bundles down there, strewn with earth, and other families crying.

That was all her mother got. A pauper's grave, without even a gravestone to mark it.

The year before, her brother John had died from

phosphorus poisoning. Matchstick-factory workers often went that way. Lizzie had saved up a few farthings for some flowers, but her father found it and spent it on drink. John was buried the same way. Another muddy pit, and a few mumbled words from a vicar who had no idea who any of them were.

Lizzie had tried to find the graves since then, but it was hopeless. There were no grand marble monuments for the dead of the London slums. They were just thrown away like so much rubbish.

Her caravan was passing the funeral procession now. Lizzie looked straight ahead. *I won't give you lot the satisfaction of rolling your eyes at me*, she thought. *You don't know what I've been through in my life.*

Victoria whinnied and shook her head. She clattered sideways for a moment, as if a horsefly had bitten her.

'Easy, girl!' Nora said, alarmed. Many of the mourners turned to stare as she struggled to calm the mare.

The casket passed through the cemetery gates. At that exact moment, Victoria reared up. Her hooves waved in the air. Someone in the crowd gave a cry of fear.

Gasps rang out as Erin leaped from her seat onto

Victoria's smooth back. Hanging on with her legs, she stroked the long mane and whispered into Victoria's ears until the horse seemed calmer.

Lizzie stole a quick glance into the cemetery and saw the casket making its way up a slope towards an open grave, where a crowd was waiting.

'Wouldn't look if I were you, Lizzie,' Nora said.

'Why not? It's only a load of toffs.'

Nora lowered her voice. 'There's something in Kensal Green Cemetery you don't want coming after you. Victoria's got wind of it.'

Lizzie laughed. 'Get away.'

'Didn't you see how spooked she was?'

'She just got worried by the big crowd, didn't she, Erin?'

Still on the horse's back, Erin didn't reply.

Nora shivered and whispered, 'They say that cemetery's haunted.'

'"They" say that about *every* cemetery,' Lizzie said scornfully.

'Not like this one. Have you not heard the rhyme?

Hide your face, my darling girl, and run, oh run for home,

For round the stones of Kensal Green, the Devil's

Hound does roam.'

'Devil's Hound, my foot!' Lizzie scoffed. Her friends could be so superstitious sometimes. 'It was the crowd that spooked her. That's all.'

'D'you think?' Nora said. 'Well, we'd best hope Victoria doesn't panic at her next sight of a crowd. We can't have her acting up like that on opening night.'

That was a frightening thought. The new horses were a big investment and Fitzy was counting on them to take part. He'd even had new posters printed, featuring the twins balancing on Albert and Victoria's backs. They *had* to be ready to perform.

Up ahead, the convoy was moving off the road and into a green field.

'We're here!' Lizzie said. 'About time. My bottom's gone numb.'

In only a few moments, the atmosphere changed from weary boredom to frantic hard work as Fitzy's Circus set about pitching its show tent. The rain was still coming down in torrents, threatening to turn the field into a muddy swamp. First the canvas and poles had to be unpacked, then the rigging and the stakes along with the mallets to drive them in. Meanwhile, enclosures had to be set up for the animals, who all needed to be fed and watered after their journey.

Like scenes from a mad poet's dream, camels trotted past behind bearded ladies, a boy with clawlike hands and feet tucked nails into his mouth and a hammer under his arm, a woman as fat as a hot air balloon passed wicker travelling baskets to her short, smiling husband, and acrobats stood on one another's shoulders to lift tent poles into position.

It looked like chaos, but Fitzy had it all under control. Lizzie loved to watch him at work, striding from place to place with his cane under his arm. If any job needed an extra pair of hands, he'd roll up his sleeves and help, never mind the mud and wet.

'Hari!' Lizzie called, running up to help the lean Indian boy lead one of the elephants out. 'Easy, Akula. It's me!' The elephant nuzzled her fondly under the arm, making her giggle.

Once Akula was safely set up with fresh hay and a meal, Lizzie went to see where else she could be useful. Her own fortune-telling tent didn't have to be put up until later.

The Boisset family, acrobats and high-wire walkers, were pulling up a support pole. Lizzie ran over to give them a hand. Dru Boisset was tall for his age, and everyone agreed he was turning into a handsome young man. 'You 'ave muscles,' he said approvingly.

'Do I?' Lizzie was a little mortified at that.

The French boy laughed. 'For a girl, I mean.'

'Try bending an iron bar next,' grunted Mario the strong man, giving her a wink.

One of the clowns, JoJo, was unloading crates stuffed with juggling clubs, costumes and props. Lizzie always looked forward to helping him, since he loved to try out new routines with her. 'Chuck 'em over here!' she joked. 'I'll catch them!'

JoJo stared. There were dark bags under his eyes. 'Are you going to give us a hand or not?'

Startled, Lizzie ran to take the other end of the crate. 'I was just joking.'

Jojo sighed and rubbed his sweating forehead. 'I know. Sorry, love. I'm not myself today.'

'What's the matter?'

He blinked helplessly, as if there was something he badly needed to say, but didn't dare to. 'I'm feeling a bit poorly,' he admitted.

'You go and lie down. I'll unload the rest of this stuff.'

'You sure?'

'Of course! Go and get some rest.' She patted JoJo on the back.

But the moment she touched him, her skin prickled all over. In her mind's eye, she saw a shadow. Long, ragged arms stretched out to grasp JoJo. It wore a hood and robe, but there was nothing beneath but bare bones. *Death.* Next second, it was gone.

Lizzie gasped and pulled away.

From somewhere in the distance – possibly from Kensal Green cemetery itself – came a long mournful howl. Lizzie's blood chilled as the sound went right through her.

It was the baying of a hound...

To find out what happens next, read
THE DEVIL'S HOUND

For more exciting books from brilliant
authors, follow the fox!
www.curious-fox.com